THE BLOODWATER MYSTERIES

skullduggery

PETE HAUTMAN
WINNER OF THE NATIONAL BOOK AWARD
AND MARY LOGUE

SLEUTH
PUTNAM

238   9548

G. P. PUTNAM'S SONS
A division of Penguin Young Readers Group.
Published by The Penguin Group.
Penguin Group (USA) Inc., 375 Hudson Street, New York, NY 10014, U.S.A.

Penguin Group (Canada), 90 Eglinton Avenue East, Suite 700, Toronto, Ontario, Canada
M4P 2Y3 (a division of Pearson Penguin Canada Inc.). Penguin Books Ltd, 80 Strand,
London WC2R 0RL, England. Penguin Ireland, 25 St. Stephen's Green, Dublin 2, Ireland
(a division of Penguin Books Ltd.). Penguin Group (Australia), 250 Camberwell Road,
Camberwell, Victoria 3124, Australia (a division of Pearson Australia Group Pty Ltd).
Penguin Books India Pvt Ltd, 11 Community Centre, Panchsheel Park, New Delhi—
110 017, India. Penguin Group (NZ), Cnr Airborne and Rosedale Roads, Albany, Auckland
1310, New Zealand (a division of Pearson New Zealand Ltd). Penguin Books (South Africa)
(Pty) Ltd, 24 Sturdee Avenue, Rosebank, Johannesburg 2196, South Africa.
Penguin Books Ltd, Registered Offices: 80 Strand, London WC2R 0RL, England.

Published simultaneously in Canada. Printed in the United States of America.
Design by Gina DiMassi. Text set in Granjon.
Library of Congress Cataloging-in-Publication Data
Hautman, Pete, 1952– Skullduggery / by Pete Hautman and Mary Logue.
p. cm. — (The Bloodwater mysteries) Summary: During a field trip in the local woods,
Roni and Brian find the local archaeology professor, Andrew Dart, knocked unconscious
in a cave, which leads them to investigate a land development scheme. [1. Real estate
development—Fiction. 2. Environmental protection—Fiction. 3. Swindlers and swindling—
Fiction. 4. Reporters and reporting—Fiction. 5. Mystery and detective stories.] I. Logue,
Mary. II. Title. PZ7.H2887Sku 2007 [Fic]—dc22 2006020576
ISBN 978-0-399-24378-3
1 3 5 7 9 10 8 6 4 2
First Impression

For Jack

contents

1
bones

Dr. Andrew Dart had climbed thirty feet up the limestone bluff when a rock struck an outcropping just above his head. Dart flinched, then looked up. He saw and heard nothing.

Dart drew a shuddering breath. Chunks of limestone, loosened by wind and rain, sometimes broke away on their own. A few inches to the right and it could have killed him.

He rested on a shallow ledge and wiped his brow. From his perch he could see over the trees to where Bloodwater River flowed into the Mississippi. Not many wild places like this left in southern Minnesota.

All this land had once been populated by Native Americans. The rivers had been their freeways. They had built great villages looking out over the Mississippi River—maybe even right here, at the top of this rocky precipice.

The bluff he was climbing, and the woodland below, were now owned by Bloodwater College, where Dart was a professor of archaeology. But in a few days the land would be sold to a developer. Dart had taken it upon himself to do a final survey of the area before the bulldozers arrived. If he could find just one good piece of archaeological evidence—the ruins of a Native American village, or a burial mound—the college might be persuaded to stop the sale. Even a single unusual artifact might be enough.

Dart resumed his climb. Moments later, he had reached the odd cleft in the rock he had seen from below. There was a concealed opening, a crack in the bluff just wide enough for a man to squeeze through. He sniffed. Bat guano. A good sign there was a cave.

He stood in the entrance and tried to get a grip on himself. He hadn't planned on exploring a cave. All he had was the small flashlight attached to his key chain. And he did not like dark places. But this was important.

He forced himself to take a few steps into the cave, then stopped and let his eyes adjust to the dark. The passageway was narrow and low. He ducked his head and followed the weak beam of his flashlight. He felt panic rise in his chest as the passage narrowed. The rock walls seemed to be closing in on him, but he forced himself to move farther into the cavern.

The passageway soon widened into a large chamber. He could hear the chittering of bats from above. Staying close to the wall, he came upon another narrow passageway leading off to the right. He saw footprints in the dust—he was not the first person to visit this cave. As he examined a footprint, he heard a shuffling noise. He froze, listening carefully, but didn't hear it again. Probably an echo.

Moving deeper into the chamber, he gasped at what he saw next. A collection of dry yellow bones lay piled against the cavern wall.

A skeleton! Was it human? Yes! He could see the skull!

He shined his flashlight into the empty eye sockets. This is just what I need! he thought.

Dart heard the shuffling sound again. He turned to look just as something smashed into the back of his head. He pitched forward, and the last thing he heard was the snapping of ancient, brittle bones.

2

blue eyes

Roni Delicata stared at Professor Bloom's face with what she hoped might be mistaken for polite attentiveness. In fact, she was merely noting how much he looked like a lady's slipper orchid, with his pouchy lower lip, pink face, bulging eyes and batlike ears. It made sense, Roni thought, since that was all the man seemed to want to talk about. Lady's slippers and trout lilies.

Yawn.

"The Bloodwater Bottoms is home to dozens of endangered wildflower species," the professor intoned, pointing to a map with his cane. "Not only lady's slippers and trout lilies, but also such rare beauties as *Latinus misbegottenus, Boringus dullemia* and *Mesmerus dozingus . . .*"

Roni shook herself awake.

"Did you have a question, young lady?" said Professor Bloom.

"Um, no . . . I just wondered if, uh . . . ." She tried to think of something—anything—interesting. "Are there any *poisonous* plants?"

"Indeed!" said the professor, rapping the hard wooden tip of his cane on the floor. "Certain mushrooms such as *Amanita virosa* and *Galerina autumnalis* can be deadly. And of course there is *Symplocarpus foetidus,* better known as skunk cabbage, which is toxic if not properly cooked. Also, the seeds of the native bindweed plant, a type of morning glory, produce a powerful hallucinogen. In addition, there are . . ." He went on with a list of long Latin names.

Looking out the corner of her eye, Roni noted that several of the other students were also struggling to stay awake. The only one who seemed at all interested was Brian Bain. That figured. Brian was fascinated by all things nerdy and scientific, no matter how boring. Fortunately, this character flaw was offset by the fact that Brian was also fascinated by explosive devices, clandestine operations and other risky behaviors.

Brian caught her looking at him and stuck out his tongue. Roni looked away. So immature. But what could you expect? Sure, he was smart enough to have gotten bumped up to the ninth grade, but he was still just a kid.

Why had she signed up for this stupid Regional Studies class? It was the middle of the summer. She should be out having fun in the sun like practically every other kid in Bloodwater. But *noooooo*! Her mother, Nick, had decided that a perfect B-minus average was not good enough for a girl of Roni's "great potential."

Potential, schmotential. If this orchid-faced nutjob kept hammering her with Latin swamp-plant names, her brain would melt into a puddle of primordial ooze.

"Aren't we supposed to go on a field trip?" another student asked.

"Indeed we are! This afternoon we will be exploring the

Bloodwater Bottoms, one of the few areas of virgin forest remaining in the county—yes, young man?"

Brian asked, "Didn't I hear something about a housing development going up in the bottoms?"

The professor scowled. "A company called Bloodwater Development wanted to build a condominium complex right along the river, which would have permanently damaged the delicate ecosystem. Totally irresponsible!" As he spoke, the professor's face turned red. He pounded his fist into his palm. "They would have destroyed the last of the trout lilies!" He paused and took a deep breath. "Fortunately, the developers decided to build their condominiums on top of Indian Bluff, rather than in the precious bottomlands."

Professor Bloom frowned, looking toward the back of the room. "Excuse me, young man, are you registered for this seminar?"

Everyone turned to look at the boy who had just walked into the classroom.

Omigod, thought Roni.

She squeezed her eyes closed, then opened them. He was still there: tall and blue eyed with curly black hair. Omigod, she whispered to herself. Blue eyes and black hair did it to her every time.

The boy looked at the sheet of paper in his hand. His dark eyebrows came together in a way that made Roni's belly go all tingly.

"Is this Regional Studies?" the boy asked.

"Indeed it is," said Professor Bloom. "You are twenty-two minutes late."

"I got lost. We just moved to town last week and I—"

"Be that as it may, arriving late to the first day of class is not an auspicious beginning."

"A not a *what?*" said the boy.

A nervous laugh erupted from Roni's throat. She couldn't stop it. It sounded like a bullfrog belching.

She clapped a hand to her mouth, but it was too late. Every single person in the classroom—including *him*—turned and stared at her. She wanted to climb under her desk and die.

"Did you say something, Miss Delicata?" asked the professor.

Roni shook her head vigorously. Her face had to be the color of a beet. Gennifer Kohlstad, two rows over, gave her a knowing smirk. Roni looked away, going from embarrassed to furious. A gorgeous guy with blue eyes and black hair would also appeal to a tart like Gennifer. Roni wouldn't have a chance against Gennifer's sexy boy-killer looks and bubbly personality.

The professor returned his attention to the new student and directed him to the nearest desk.

"What is your name, son?"

"Eric." The boy smiled. "Eric Bloodwater."

3
curses

Bloodwater? Brian Bain twisted his neck to get a better look at the kid, who had sat at a desk near the back of the room. Eric Bloodwater leaned forward in his seat, as if looking attentive would make up for his late arrival.

Nobody named Bloodwater had lived in Bloodwater for nearly fifty years. And *those* Bloodwaters . . . well, they'd pretty much gone insane and killed each other off. In fact, every Bloodwater Brian had ever heard of had come to a bad end.

Some people said there was a Bloodwater Curse. Curse or no, the Bloodwaters were ancient history. Brian had always assumed that the whole clan had died out years ago.

But this kid did not look dead. Or cursed.

"Mr. Bain, would you mind directing your attention to the front of the room?" asked Professor Bloom.

"Sorry," Brian said, looking back at the professor.

"As I was explaining for Mr. Bloodwater's benefit, today we are studying the plant life endemic to Bloodwater Bottoms and the surrounding area. Later this week, Dr. Andrew Wyndham Dart will visit us to talk about Native American archaeology in the region. We will also learn about Bloodwater politics and government, which will include a visit to the county courthouse and jail.

"Now, as I was saying, a number of rare plant species can be found in the hardwood forests along the lower Bloodwater . . ."

Brian sneaked a look at Roni Delicata, a few rows over. He hadn't seen much of her lately. Actually, not since they'd gotten themselves in a world of trouble by investigating—and solving—the Alicia Camden kidnapping. That had been fun. Dangerous, but fun.

Brian wouldn't have minded hanging out with Roni more, but they didn't really have much in common. He was three years younger than her. He was smart about science stuff; she didn't care if the earth was round, flat or triangular. She was a reporter for the school paper; he belonged to the Robot Club and the Chess Club. She was good at talking to people; he always stuck his foot in his mouth. About the only thing they had in common was that they both liked solving crimes. Without a crime, they just didn't have much to talk about.

Roni kept sneaking looks toward the back of the room. What was she looking at? Brian followed her glance and decided she was looking at Eric Bloodwater.

Uh-oh, he thought. That could mean two things.

Either she'd developed an instant crush, or she'd found herself another mystery.

Or both.

4
skunk cabbage

Professor Bloom said they'd head out for their first field trip after lunch to search for lady's slipper orchids, trout lilies and skunk cabbage.

Skunk cabbage? Roni couldn't imagine why anyone would want to find such a horridly named specimen. She found a place to sit on the low brick wall outside the school and opened her container of peach yogurt. The yogurt was disgusting and the wall was uncomfortable, but she had a perfect view of Eric Bloodwater, who was sitting by himself with his back against the trunk of a small tree.

Maybe she should go over and sit down next to him. Ask him a really interesting question to show him how smart and fascinating she was. Either that or just smile and simper and gaze at him adoringly, which was what most guys seemed to want.

Roni forced down another spoonful of the sickeningly sweet peach yogurt. She had an olive loaf sandwich in her bag, but she didn't want Eric to see her shoving a huge sandwich down her throat. The yogurt seemed more elegant.

She stole another look at Eric Bloodwater and sighed. He was just *too* good-looking. She didn't have a chance. Not unless she instantly dropped fifteen pounds. And her legs grew a couple of inches. And . . . what was she thinking? She was who she was. Roni Delicata, teenage shlump.

On the other hand, she had nothing to lose. If he told her to get lost, at least she could stop thinking about him. Maybe.

"Whatcha staring at, Sherlock?"

Roni jumped.

"Don't *do* that!" she snapped at Brian, who had sneaked up behind her. She gave him her best glare, but Brian, in his eternal Brianly way, didn't seem to notice. He sat down on the wall beside her, his broad, open, Korean face smiling.

"Isn't this class great?" he said.

"Sure, if you like being bored out of your skull. I'm not here by choice."

"You flunk a class?"

Roni looked around, making sure that no one else could hear her. "No, I didn't flunk anything, but my mom thought my grades could be improved."

"Cool."

"No, Brian, it isn't cool. It's pathetic. I have much more important things I could be doing with my summer."

"Name one."

"How about sleeping till noon? Instead of tramping around in the woods looking for skunk cabbage. You don't think he's gonna make us eat it, do you?"

Brian laughed. "You kidding? *Symplocarpus foetidus* is poisonous!"

"You spout one more Latin name I'm going to pour this yogurt over your head."

Professor Bloom appeared at the door of the school. He hung his cane over his forearm and clapped his hands.

"People! People! Gather 'round, please!"

Brian and Roni walked up to him together. He pointed at them. "You two are a pair." Then he proceeded to pair off the rest of the class. To Roni's horror, he put Gennifer with Eric.

"We will be using the buddy system when we're in the bottoms this afternoon. Stick with your partner and try to avoid sinkholes, bogs, stinging nettles, poison ivy, rattlesnakes and other potential sources of discomfort. You will each be assigned a particular species, choosing from the list of plants I handed out at the beginning of class. Think of it as a sort of scavenger hunt."

Brian's hand shot up. "Can Roni and I have skunk cabbage?"

Roni felt her face turning pink. Why had she let the little twit even walk next to her? Now she was stuck with him—and skunk cabbage—for the rest of the day.

5

help!

"I thought you were interested in skunk cabbage," Brian said. "It being poisonous and all . . ."

Roni made a growling noise in her throat. Brian could tell her heart wasn't in their assignment. When she was interested in finding something, she could put a bloodhound to shame. But she wasn't even really looking. She was just walking through the woods with a scowl on her face, complaining about the nettles and jumping every time she saw a stick that looked like a snake. She could have tripped over a skunk cabbage and never noticed it.

He decided not to pay much attention to her. Let her get over it by herself. Brian loved wandering in the woods. He wanted to know the names of everything—animal, vegetable or mineral.

"What's *that* abominable blob?" she asked, pointing at a gelatinous, orange globule perched on top of a fallen log.

"Slime mold, I think," said Brian.

"Yuck. Is it on our list?"

"I don't think so."

"Good."

Brian stopped and took in their surroundings. "This might not be a good place to find skunk cabbage," he said. "According to Professor Bloom, they like really wet soil."

"This is wet enough," Roni said. She looked up the sloping hillside. "It looks like easier walking up there. Less itchweed."

"Less skunk cabbage, too."

"How do you tell a skunk cabbage, anyway? All these plants look the same."

"Well, for one thing, it smells sort of skunky."

"Great. Let's make it a point to not find any." Without waiting for him to reply, Roni headed uphill.

"We're supposed to stay together!" Brian said.

"Come on then," she said over her shoulder.

Brian sighed. Hanging with Roni was like trying to walk a bull elephant. He scrambled to catch up with her, giving up on the notion of locating a stand of skunk cabbage. Maybe something else would turn up.

About twenty yards up the slope they came to a grassy area. Above them rose the limestone cliff known as Indian Bluff. He followed Roni along the base of the bluff.

Brian asked, "So what do you think about that Eric Bloodwater?"

Roni's head snapped around and her face went pink. "What do you mean by that?"

"Nothing," Brian said. "I just think it's pretty weird that he would have the same name as the town."

"The city was *named* after the Bloodwater family, my dear Watson."

"Yeah, but there hasn't been a Bloodwater in Bloodwater since forever. I thought the whole family had died out."

"Probably just some distant relatives."

"I guess. Hey, do you suppose they're the ones who are renting out Bloodwater House?"

"Somebody's living there again?"

"Yeah. My mom mentioned something about it. The bank is renting it to some family. I wonder if the Curse will get them."

Roni shook her head and continued walking. "You and your stupid Curse." She waded through a patch of green three-leafed plants. Brian stopped. It looked like poison ivy. He opened his mouth to tell Roni what she'd just done, but before he could say anything, she held up a hand and said, "Did you hear that?"

Brian listened, but heard only the breeze. "Hear what?"

Roni held up her hand. "Listen."

They both listened. A bird calling . . . the muted drone of a distant airplane . . . and then a faint but unmistakable call for help.

6

sweetie pie

"Where's it coming from?" Brian asked.

"Shh!" Roni cocked her head, listening fiercely. She had heard the voice call out twice, but she couldn't locate it.

Several seconds passed.

"Help!"

"There it is again!" Brian said. He looked up the rocky face of the cliff. "Up there!"

"Up where?" Roni looked up at the bluff, but saw nothing but a craggy wall of rock.

Brian was already climbing. Roni took a deep breath and followed.

It was easier than it looked. The rock provided plenty of handholds and crevices. As long as she didn't look down, it wasn't bad at all. About thirty feet up, she came to a shallow ledge. Brian was waiting for her.

"I heard it again," he said. "It sounded like it was coming right out of the rock. Come on!" Brian edged along the narrow ledge. "Watch out for snakes," he added.

"That is not funny."

"Wasn't meant to be."

The ledge narrowed, and Roni's toes were hanging out over the edge. She made the mistake of looking down. Her stomach did a flip-flop. It was only about thirty feet, but it looked like a mile.

Again, they heard the voice, still faint but louder than before. *"Hello? Can anybody hear me?"*

"Up here," Brian said, and he was climbing again. Roni followed him up to another ledge.

"Hey!" he said. And then he seemed to melt into the rock.

Roni did not like being halfway up a cliff, and especially not alone. She slowly inched along the ledge until she came to a hidden opening, a slash in the rock about five feet high and twelve inches wide. The air coming out of it was cool and sour smelling.

"Brian?" she called out.

There was no answer.

The cave widened a few yards past the entrance. Brian congratulated himself for having a flashlight with him. True, it was a tiny thing, its beam of light no more powerful than a candle, but it was better than no light at all.

The flashlight was one of several pieces of equipment Brian liked to have on his person. The other necessities in his numerous pockets included a small 10x magnifying glass, a Swiss Army knife, a short spool of copper wire, a six-foot tape measure and several pieces of hard candy. Because you never knew when you might get caught in the dark with nothing to eat.

As he moved deeper into the cave, he noticed that the sour smell was getting stronger. He also noticed several sets of footprints on the dusty floor. He stopped and called out.

"Anybody in here?" His voice echoed weirdly off the limestone walls. A few heartbeats later a querulous voice came from deeper within the cavern.

"Help! I can't find the light switch."

Light switch?

"I'm coming!" Brian said.

The voice sounded fainter than before. Brian wondered how they had ever heard it from outside the cave. Some strange amplification effect, he supposed. Caverns did odd things to sounds. Following the twisting passageway, Brian noticed his flashlight beam getting weaker. How long had it been since he had replaced the battery? Too long.

The passageway opened into a large chamber. The smell was stronger, and he could see why. The floor was black with bat droppings.

Brian shined his light up and was rewarded with an outburst of angry chittering. Hundreds of bats hung from the ceiling twenty feet above his head.

He heard the disembodied voice again. "Where am I?" After a moment, the voice answered itself: "Why, I'm right here! Of course I'm here. Where else would I be?"

Brian shone his light in the direction of the voice and saw a low opening to his right. He ducked his head and crawled through into another chamber. Just as he entered the new chamber, his light gave out.

Brian stood up slowly, blinking his eyes in the utter blackness. There is no dark darker than the darkness inside a cave, he decided.

He could hear someone breathing, and then the voice again, very close.

"Is that you, Sweetie Pie?"

7

yorick

Roni peered into the cave entrance. She thought she could hear faint voices.

"Brian?" she called again.

"Back here!" His voice echoed through the passageway.

She took a few steps into the narrow opening.

Maybe whoever was in there was holding Brian captive, forcing him to lure her into a fiendish trap. An escaped convict. Or a cave troll. You never knew.

As her eyes adjusted to the dark, she could make out the faint outlines of the cavern walls, but the deeper it went the less she could see. She took another step. The passage curved to the right and led into complete darkness.

Roni plopped her backpack on the floor of the cave and rooted around in it. Her mom laughed at her for having so much junk in her backpack, but as she liked to say, you never knew what might come in handy. She found the lavender-scented mood candle she had bought a few days ago. In one of the side pockets she located a really cute box of matches she had nabbed from Bratten's Café and Bakery.

She lit the candle and held it out in front of her. Not much light, but enough to let her see where she was going. "I'm coming," she yelled.

As the passageway opened into a chamber, she heard an

odd beeping sound, like someone's cell phone put on hyper-speed. She looked up and almost dropped her candle. At first she thought the ceiling was alive. Then she *knew* it was alive. Alive with bats. They covered the ceiling like thick, leathery, wriggling carpeting.

Roni wondered if they were disturbed by the candlelight. Too bad, she thought, I gotta see. She forced herself to enter the chamber, making a promise to herself that she would make Brian pay for this. She would have him tortured and killed. Why had he left her side? What good was a sidekick if they weren't there to kick when you needed them?

She tried calling again. "Brian!"

"Here," a thin voice squeaked out of an opening in the far wall.

She crossed to the opening. It was low and narrow. She would have to crawl. What if she got stuck? How embarrassing would that be? She didn't like tight places; they made her feel squeamy.

"Come out," she shouted.

"I can't see! My flashlight died!"

She held out the candle. "Can you see my light?"

"Yes! But I need your help."

"Help doing what?" she asked.

"There's a guy in here. I think he's hurt."

Roni wished that she and Brian had a secret word they could say when they were in serious trouble to let the other one know to run as fast as they could and get help and not enter the scary other chamber. But they didn't.

"Hurry up!" Brian said.

Roni ducked her head and crawled into the opening, holding the candle in front of her. A few seconds later the passageway opened into a chamber, and she was able to stand up.

"I love it!" Brian said when he saw her. "A candle! How nineteenth century."

"At least the batteries don't give out."

Brian pointed down and Roni saw a thin, bearded man slumped against the wall. He looked like he was about her mom's age. His eyes were closed.

"Is he alive?"

"Yeah, but he's not making much sense."

Roni knelt down next to the man. "What happened?"

The man's eyes popped open. "Sweetie Pie?" he said in a quavering voice. "Is that you?"

Roni looked at Brian. "Sweetie Pie?"

"He calls everybody that," Brian said. "He's a little out of it."

Roni noticed a trail of dried blood winding down the man's neck. She bent closer to him and saw that he had a large cut on the back of his head.

"What happened to your head?" she asked.

"Somebody hit me."

"Who?"

"It must have been a ghost," said the man.

Roni stood up straight. "Oh, great. A ghost."

"Or maybe a skinwalker," he said.

"What's a skinwalker?" Brian asked.

"An evil shape-changing shaman."

"Oh. I'll take the ghost," said Brian.

"Can you get up?" Roni asked. "Can you walk?"

"I could if everything would stop spinning."

"What's that he's sitting on?" Roni asked. It looked like a pile of oddly shaped yellow sticks. She moved the candle closer, then gasped. "It's *bones!*"

"Bonesy bonesy bonesy," the man cackled. He brought up his right hand, holding a human skull.

Roni let out a yelp and jumped back.

"Alas, poor Yorick! I knew him, Horatio!" The man laughed, then suddenly became very serious. "Whatever you do," he said, looking straight at Roni, "don't let them eat your brains."

8

bulldozers and ghosts

"You stay with him," Roni said. "I'll go get help."

"Okay," Brian said. "Except how about if *I* go for help, and *you* stay."

"I don't think so," said Roni.

"Let's flip a coin," Brian suggested.

"You should stay. You've known him longer."

"I don't actually know him that well," said Brian.

The man held up the skull and said, "He can *hear* you."

Roni said, "Let's compromise. We both go back to the entrance, then you can have the candle and come back here to keep him company while I get help."

"That's a compromise?"

"Yup."

As usual, Roni got her way. Brian walked her out of the cave, then returned with the candle to keep the mad-man company.

The guy had the skull again and was staring into its empty eye sockets. He said, "Bloodwater owes you a debt of gratitude, Yorick. You have saved us from ourselves."

"If you keep talking to that skull, I'm going to leave you here," Brian said.

For several seconds, the man said nothing. Then he asked, "Are you going to get me out of here?"

Finally, he had said something that made sense.

"My friend went to get help."

"Good."

"What's your name?" Brian asked.

"I am Dart," said the man. "Andrew Dart. Dr. Andrew Dart. Andrew Wyndham Dart, PhD. I am an archaeologist. I work at Bloodwater College."

"Dr. Dart? I think you're supposed to talk to my class!"

"I'm afraid I may have to cancel—I have more important work to do!"

"Why were you in here?" Brian asked.

"I came to stop the bulldozers," said Dr. Dart. He reached out and grabbed Brian's wrist. "You have to help me!"

"I am helping you. My friend—"

"No! I mean you must help me stop the bulldozers!" His eyes glittered in the candlelight, sane and sober. "Indian Bluff is one of the greatest archaeological sites ever discovered in the area. We can't let them destroy it!" Then he whispered, "But don't breathe a word of this to Jillian!"

"Um . . . okay. Don't tell Jillian. Right. Could you please let go of my arm?"

Dr. Dart placed Brian's hand on top of the skull. "Swear on Yorick. If anything should happen to me, you must save the bluff!"

"Save the bluff. Uh-huh."

"You swear?"

"Sure . . . whatever."

Dr. Dart released his grip. Brain wiped his hand on his shirt. He had never touched a human skull before.

"They didn't believe me," Dr. Dart said. He reached into his shirt pocket and came out with something wrapped in a handkerchief. With shaking hands, he unfolded the cloth to reveal a flat, palm-sized stone. He held the stone out to Brian. "Take it."

"What is it?"

"Take it!"

Clearly, this Andrew Dart was raving. Brian took the stone quickly so that Dart couldn't grab his arm again, and put it in his pocket.

"No matter what happens to me, you must save the bluff. I have enemies!" He looked over Brian's shoulder and his eyes suddenly went wide.

Brian whirled and held up the candle—but there was nothing there.

"They sneak up on you," said Dart.

"Who?" Brian's heart was pounding.

"The ghosts," Dart said. "The bulldozers and the ghosts."

9

eric bloodwater

Roni pointed the way up the bluff for the two paramedics. She stood below and watched them climb the bluff and enter the cave. By that time, Professor Bloom's entire class had gathered in a clearing about fifty feet back from the base of the bluff.

"Is there really somebody in there?" Adam, one of Brian's nerdy friends, asked.

"Yeah," Roni said. "We heard him yelling for help, so Brian and I went in and found him."

"That is so cool!"

Roni was pleased. It *was* cool, not to mention courageous and brave. Her mother would probably add reckless and foolish to the mix. But that was cool, too.

After a few minutes, Brian emerged from the cave. He climbed down the bluff, walked up to Roni and said, "You took long enough."

"I was on the bus driver's cell phone five minutes after I left you."

"It felt like forever."

"Sorry. I wonder who he is."

"His name is Dr. Andrew Dart. He's the archaeologist who was supposed to talk to our class."

"You actually got him to make sense?"

"Just for a minute. He made me swear to stop the bulldozers. He says the bluff is an important Indian site or something. Then he started talking about ghosts and stuff."

A large, bony hand descended on her shoulder.

"Come along, Miss Delicata," said Professor Bloom. "It's time for us to return to school and let the rescue workers do their job."

"Can't I stay and watch? It was me and Brian who found him."

"I am aware of that. You were supposed to be looking for skunk cabbage. What were you doing way up here?"

"We thought we smelled something skunky."

"Perhaps it was a skunk. Now come along."

The rest of the group, including Brian, were already walking toward the bus. Roni shrugged and followed them.

When they got on the bus, Roni did not sit with Brian. She didn't want anyone—especially Eric Bloodwater—to think that she and Brian were boyfriend and girlfriend. Maybe when Eric got on he would sit next to her. She looked around discreetly. Where was he?

Professor Bloom stood at the front of the bus and did a head count, using his cane as a pointer. He finished, frowned and counted them again.

"One missing. Does anyone know who that would be?"

Roni knew. It was Eric Bloodwater. But she was not about to publicly admit that she was aware of his existence.

"It's the new kid," somebody from the back yelled. "The one who came in late."

Professor Bloom consulted his notebook.

"Miss Kohlstad?"

"Yes?" said Gennifer Kohlstad.

"Where is Mr. Bloodwater, your partner?"

"He wandered off, I guess."

Several of the students snickered.

"And when did this event occur?"

"Pretty much right away. I mean, I haven't seen him since we first went into the woods."

Professor Bloom made an exasperated *pffftt* sound. "It seems we have a missing person, people. This is exactly the sort of inconvenient situation I had hoped to avert by employing the buddy system. Inconvenient for all of us, I might add. Now we are going to have to—"

"Hey!" said Eric Bloodwater, climbing into the bus. "You weren't going to leave without me, were you?"

Eric plopped down right next to Brian. Roni couldn't believe it. She had a seat free, but he had walked right past her. Maybe he'd sat next to Brian because Brian was a boy. Some guys were like that.

At least he hadn't sat by Gennifer Kohlstad. In fact, Gennifer seemed to be pointedly ignoring Eric.

Eric and Brian were one row back and across the aisle from Roni. She turned her head so she could hear them.

Eric asked Brian, "So what was going on up by the bluff? I saw a bunch of rescue workers hauling some guy out of a cave."

Brian told Eric about the cave, and how they had found the injured archaeologist. "He sustained a head injury, which may have caused dementia and loss of motor function."

Roni could tell Brian wasn't sure about Eric. His level of language elevated when he wanted to put someone off.

But Eric wasn't put off. He laughed and said, "Oh, you mean like he went wacko."

"I guess so. He was raving about ghosts. And about stopping the bulldozers."

"Stop the dozers?" Eric frowned. "How did he expect to do that?"

Roni leaned into the aisle. "He said he'd been attacked."

Eric looked at her. "You talked to him, too?"

"We both went in the cave," Roni said. "There was a skeleton in there."

"Wow." He grinned, showing big white teeth that were just ever-so-slightly crooked. Roni felt her heart turning to mush.

Eric said, "I thought this class was going to be beyond boring, but you guys are managing to liven it up."

Brian beamed. "We do our best."

Roni leaned closer to Eric and lowered her voice. "What happened with you and Gennifer?"

Eric rolled his eyes. "I ditched her. She was too slow and too talky. Besides, I wanted to check out the land on top of the bluff. It's all going to be my dad's property pretty soon."

Professor Bloom, who apparently had very sharp hearing, turned in his seat and thumped his cane on the floor of the bus. "Not *all* of it, young man. The bottoms are safe from your father's predations."

Eric sat back. "Well, maybe not the bottoms, but he's buying the bluff and the land up above. The bulldozers will be there in a few days." Eric turned to Brian. "And that cave you found? That's going to be *my* cave."

10

red bumps

"That's the scoop, Nick," Roni said to her mom as they both picked away at a salad. "Just another ordinary day with madmen and skeletons." The salad had too much lettuce in it as far as Roni was concerned. Not enough artichoke hearts and chicken. She added another glob of bleu cheese dressing and mixed it into the relentless mound of green.

"That's quite a story. I hope the poor man is okay," her mother said. "Will you be writing about it for the paper?"

"The school newspaper doesn't come out in the summer."

"Maybe you should get a job with the *Clarion*."

Roni sat up straight. "That's a great idea."

"*After* you finish school."

"Oh." Roni deflated. She reached down to scratch her ankle. Must be a mosquito bite, she thought. "Hey, what's the deal with Indian Bluff? Is it true that they're putting in condos?"

"Yes. A man named Fred Bloodwater is building a development there."

"His son is in my class! I thought all the Bloodwaters were dead."

"Mr. Bloodwater just moved here with his wife and children. They've been living in California. He is the great-grandson of Augustus Bloodwater, who was the nephew of Zebulon Bloodwater, our city's founder." Nick smiled. "You'll never guess where they're staying."

"Bloodwater House?"

"Precisely."

"Do they know about the Curse?" Roni didn't really believe in the Curse of Bloodwater House, but she knew it would tweak her mother.

"Now Roni!" Nick put on her stern face. "I don't want you spreading stories, and I *especially* do not want you uttering the word *curse* in the same breath as *Bloodwater House*." Nick Delicata was the secretary to the mayor of Bloodwater. She knew more about running Bloodwater than anybody, and she was as tough as nails when it came to defending her city's reputation.

"Okay, okay. I won't freak out the new victims. I mean owners." Roni rubbed her ankles together. Now they were both itching. Maybe she was allergic to something.

"See that you don't. As for the area where you found that unfortunate man this afternoon, Mr. Bloodwater's development company is buying the land from Bloodwater College. They're selling it to raise money for a new football stadium. In fact, the city is investing considerable money in the project."

"I heard they're going to bulldoze everything and put up about a million condos."

Nick carefully chewed her final bite of salad, then pushed her plate away. "That's an exaggeration. I hate to see such a big development going in on that beautiful piece of land, too. But the mayor thinks we need this kind of growth. Actually, the original plan was to build the condos down in the bottoms to give the owners river access."

"That's virgin territory," Roni said.

"Whatever does that mean?" Nick asked as she took their plates to the sink.

"You know, a whole ecosystem that's the way it's always been."

"Nothing is the way it's always been."

"Oh, Mom, don't go and get so philosophical on me. There are plants and animals there that can't live anyplace else."

"I doubt that."

"Try the trout lily."

"Is that a plant or a fish?"

"A plant. A plant that only grows for about a three-mile stretch along the Bloodwater River. In the whole world." Until that moment, Roni could not have cared less about the trout lily, but suddenly she was passionate about saving a plant she had never even seen. Just the idea of plunking a big ugly condo down on top of a tiny defenseless wildflower was enough to make her mad.

"As I was saying," said Nick, "the plan has changed. Your trout lilies are safe. The development is going in up on the bluff. It will bring in a lot of tax money. The sale will be final this Friday. They'll break ground the same day. Fred Bloodwater will unveil his plan in a public meeting tomorrow."

"Professor Bloom is taking our class to his presentation."

"I thought Professor Bloom was a plant specialist."

"He wants us to see democracy in action. But I still think the development is a bad idea. Condos are ugly. And what if that archaeologist is right, and the bluff is an Indian burial ground or something?"

"What archaeologist?"

"The man we found in the cave! Didn't you listen to anything I said?"

"You didn't tell me he was an archaeologist. In any case, my understanding is that the area has been carefully surveyed, and that no artifacts have been found."

"Not according to Dr. Dart."

"Dart? Andrew Dart? That was who you found in the cave?"

"That's him."

"Hmm. You know, Dr. Dart has been opposed to this development from the beginning. But he hasn't found any evidence that it's worth preserving."

"He has now. The skeleton! What if it's a million-year-old Indian?"

Nick laughed. "You never exaggerate, do you!"

"What if Dr. Dart found the proof he needed to stop the development, and that's why he was attacked and left for dead!"

"Roni! What makes you think the poor man was attacked?"

"He said so."

"And who did he say attacked him?"

Roni mumbled something.

"I didn't get that," said Nick.

"A ghost. He said he was attacked by a ghost."

Nick smiled and shook her head. "Why does everything have to be such a drama with you? The man probably just bonked his head on a stalagtite."

"Maybe, but if that skeleton turns out to be really ancient, wouldn't that stop the development?"

She reached down and began scratching vigorously at her ankles.

Nick looked thoughtful. "I suppose the skeleton will have to be investigated, but—why are you scratching yourself?"

"Because I itch?"

"Let me see."

Roni swung her legs out from beneath the table, and both she and her mother gasped.

Her ankles were completely covered with tiny red bumps.

11

artifact

Brian sat in front of his computer, playing two games of speed chess at the same time. One guy he was playing called himself Dark King and lived in Germany. The other guy was from New York. His name was Jepper, whatever that meant. Brian called himself Bloodbath. He loved his name. He felt like it was strong and forceful and conveyed just the right amount of cruelty.

He had Jepper on the run, but Dark King was kicking his butt.

He heard the crunch of tires on gravel and looked out the window. It was his mom, driving her slightly battered BPD cruiser. Some kids might find it embarrassing to always have a police car in the driveway, but Brian liked it. He thought it was cool that his mom was a cop.

A few minutes later, his mom stopped outside his open door and knocked on the frame. She was always very respectful of his space.

"Playing chess again?" she said. "It's so nice outside."

"Mom, I was outside all day long, tromping around in the woods."

"Oh, right. How was your class?"

As soon as Brian made his next move, he saw that he

would be checkmated in three moves. He resigned without waiting to see what Dark King would do next.

"It's fun. Roni's taking it, too."

"Oh, Roni Delicata."

He could hear the coolness in his mother's voice. Roni hadn't really started off on the right foot with his mom, what with getting Brian into more trouble than he was capable of getting himself into—which was a lot.

"Yeah. Today we went looking for skunk cabbage, but ended up finding a crazy guy, a dead guy and about a million bats."

Mrs. Bain took a breath and let it out slowly.

"So that was you! I should have known!"

As a detective for the Bloodwater Police Department, she would already know all about the rescue.

"Yeah. Roni and I heard this guy yelling from inside a cave and—"

"And you just decided to go in after him? Brian, why didn't you just go for help? Caving is definitely not on my list of Approved Activities."

"Sorry, Mom," Brian said. "Things happened kind of fast. Just a sec. Let me polish off this Jepper guy." He moved his queen, forcing Jepper to defend his king, then advanced his knight for checkmate. Jepper messaged him "good game" and signed off.

"I don't know how you kids can be so smart and so stupid all at the same time," said Mrs. Bain.

"Me neither," said Brian. "Have you heard if Dr. Dart—the guy from the cave—is going to be okay?"

"He's at Mercy Hospital. As far as I know, he's going to be fine."

"What about the skeleton? Are you going to investigate?"

She sat down on the edge of his bed. "We spoke with the paramedics, Brian. They said they saw some old animal bones, that's all."

"But there was a human skull!"

"A skull? Are you sure?"

"Of course I'm sure!"

"Hmm. We may have to look into that. The archaeologists from the college will no doubt be interested."

"Dr. Dart is an archaeologist!"

"Then I suppose he'll want to go right back into that cave when he recovers."

"What about whoever hit Dr. Dart?"

"Hit him? What makes you say that?"

"He told me he was attacked. By a ghost."

Mrs. Bain laughed and stood up. "Brian, the man was delirious. He was lost in that cave for hours. He could have caused his own injury in any number of ways."

"Or he could really have been attacked."

"Why would anyone want to attack him?"

"He told me he had enemies. He wants to stop that development from going in on Indian Bluff."

Mrs. Bain shook her head, then started picking up dirty clothes off his floor. She was one of those people who always had to stay busy.

"We will certainly talk to him. Perhaps by tomorrow the man will start making sense. In the meantime, I don't want you spreading stories."

"But you're going to investigate?"

"We will talk to Dr. Dart."

She began to empty the pockets of Brian's cargo pants onto the bed: dead flashlight, magnifying glass, Swiss Army knife, copper wire, tape measure, candy wrappers, wallet and several other odds and ends—including the stone Dr. Dart had given him in the cave. Brian had forgotten all about it.

"I can't believe all the junk you carry around in your pockets," she said, tossing the emptied pants onto the over-flowing laundry basket. "I guess I'll do the wash." She hefted the basket and went clomping down the stairs.

Brian rolled his chair over to the bed and looked at the stone. The pale, glassy-looking rock was about five inches long, leaf shaped, pointed at both ends, with two shallow notches near one of the points. Brian held it up to the light. The edges were scalloped like the edge of a bread knife, and very sharp. Brian scraped the edge across the back of his arm. It took the hair off like a razor blade.

This was no ordinary rock.

"Hey, Dad, do you know what this is?"

Bruce Bain, Brian's father, poked his head out from behind the towers of books weighing down his cluttered desk. Lately he had been working on a book about the mating behavior of legless South American amphibians, and his office was even messier than usual.

"Hello, son. What do you have there?"

"I think it might be an Indian arrowhead."

"Indian? Are you referring to the people of India, or do you mean Native American?"

"Native American. What do you think?"

Mr. Bain put on his reading glasses and examined the stone. "A type of quartzite, I believe. Most definitely an artifact. Rather large for an arrowhead, I would say. Possibly a spear point. How did you come by it, son?"

"Somebody gave it to me. How old do you think it is?"

Mr. Bain unfolded his long, lanky body and reached up to the top shelf of the bookcase behind his desk—one of several bookcases lining the walls of the room. He pulled down an enormous leather-clad volume titled *Projectile Points of the Great Lakes Region*.

"Here you go, son," he said, handing the book to Brian, who staggered under its weight.

As Brian lugged the huge book back to his bedroom, he ran into his mother.

"My goodness, what do you have there?"

"I asked Dad one simple question and he gave me a week's worth of reading."

12

fuzzy logic

Dr. Andrew Dart knew he wasn't thinking clearly. Something had happened to his head. The room swam in and out of view. Most of the time he knew he was in a hospital, but sometimes he found himself back in the cave.

The cave! The cave was the answer. The cave had everything he needed to stop the bulldozers. He would be a hero!

A face swam into view. Yellow bone. Empty eye sockets. Gaping jaw.

The jawbone was moving in the face, up and down, like in a cartoon, then started talking. "You awakened me, white man."

"I'm sorry," said Dart. "It was an accident. But we need you now. Only you can save the land."

"You are all fools, white man. Mad, destructive fools."

"I know," said Dart. "Believe me, I know!"

"Is Andrew Dart on this ward?" Jillian Greystone asked the nurse on 3B.

"Yes he is, but I'm not sure he's up for company."

"I'm his ... fiancée. Is it okay if I just peek in on him?"

The nurse hardly looked up from her work. "I think that would be fine. But if he's sleeping, don't wake him up. You'll find him in room 313."

Jillian squared her shoulders. She was afraid he wouldn't want to see her—not after their last conversation. But she had to see him. As for being Andrew's fiancée . . . it wasn't true. Not anymore.

She walked down the hall and looked into room 313.

Andrew Dart was stretched out in a hospital bed with only a thin blanket over him. She could see his pale blue hospital gown. His head was tilted back; his eyes were closed. An IV tube fed into his right arm. Why was he on an IV? She moved closer, almost touching the bed.

He looked so pale. Andrew always pushed himself too hard. Wouldn't take a moment to enjoy life. That had been one of their problems.

The last time she had talked to him they had argued. A horrible, screaming argument. Jillian shuddered, recalling the things he had said. Andrew could be a hateful man. He cared more for his dead Indians than he did for her. Maybe he deserved to get bonked on the head.

She was glad he was alive. But she was also glad he would now have to give up his ridiculous campaign to stop the development on Indian Bluff. The construction would begin any day now, and there was nothing he could do about it. Maybe then he would focus on his other work—and on her.

She had never seen him so motionless. He looked so vulnerable lying there.

Andrew Dart's eyes snapped open.

"Sweetie Pie? Is that you?"

Jillian looked into his eyes and forced herself to smile.

"Yes, Andrew," she said. "It's me."

13

turkey tail

"You'll never guess what I've got in my hand," Brian said.

"A telephone?"

"My *other* hand."

"Never mind that. How are your legs?" Roni asked.

"Let me check." Brian looked down at his legs. "Still attached."

"I mean, do they itch?"

"No. Why?"

"Mine are completely covered with poison ivy."

"Oh!" Brian suddenly remembered seeing Roni wade through the patch of poison ivy at the base of the bluff. He had meant to tell her so she could give herself a good scrubbing when she got home, but then they'd heard Dr. Dart calling for help, and things had started happening, and it had slipped his mind. "I did see some poison ivy out there," he said. "You must have walked through it."

"I'm afraid it's terminal," Roni said.

"Don't die just yet. I have something to show you."

"I can't believe how much this itches."

"I have a suggestion."

"What? Calamine lotion? Hot compresses? Amputation?"

"Dairy Queen."

Roni didn't say anything.

"Hot fudge sundae," Brian added.

After a couple more seconds, Roni said, "I guess it can't hurt."

After the unfortunate demise of Roni's pink bicycle, Imelda, Nick had helped Roni buy a used Vespa motor scooter.

Roni loved her scooter. She had named it Hillary after Hillary Clinton, who had a lot of spunk and just kept on going. A lot of people said Hillary Clinton was too pushy. Too pushy? Roni thought. How are you supposed to get anywhere in this world if you don't shove once in a while?

Roni careened into a spot right next to the Dairy Queen. Brian was waiting for her with his skateboard under his arm. He mainly carried the thing around. Brian wasn't very coordinated, but occasionally he would push himself along on a nice flat stretch of sidewalk.

Brian patted the Vespa's front fender as if it were a dog. "How's good old Hill?" he asked.

"She's toodling along just fine, thank you very much."

"I waited for you to order."

"How thoughtful!"

"Actually, I'm kind of broke. I was hoping you'd buy."

"Figures," said Roni.

They stood in line behind a family of five kids who were ordering dinner.

"What are you getting?" she asked him. Brian was variable. He ordered as the mood struck him. Roni had two things she liked. She was always torn between them—a hot fudge sundae with whipped cream and nuts, or a chocolate dip cone with sprinkles.

"I'm going for the Three Musketeers Blizzard," he said. "Or maybe a banana split."

"Since I'm on a diet I'm just going to get a small—"

Before she could finish Brian butted in, "—chocolate dip cone with sprinkles."

Roni laughed. "Precisely, Watson."

"Hey, nice socks!"

"Socks?" Roni looked down at her legs. They were bright pink from ankles to knees. "That's calamine lotion," she said. "For my poison ivy."

"I was just kidding."

"Thanks a lot. I'd actually forgotten about it for ten seconds. Now it itches like crazy."

"Think chocolate dip cone with sprinkles," Brian said.

Amazingly, as soon as she started thinking about ice cream again, the itching subsided.

They both ordered. Brian changed his mind at the last second and got a Buster Bar. They brought their ice cream over to a picnic table and sat down. After the first bite, Brian reached into his pocket and handed her a flat, whitish stone.

"What does this mean? Are we going steady?" she asked.

He cracked up. Roni had to smile. One of the things that made Brian tolerable was that he thought she was funny.

Roni took a closer look at the stone. "Is this like an Indian thing?" she asked.

"Very good, Watson."

"You're Watson; I'm Holmes. Where'd you get it?"

"Dr. Dart gave it to me. I just figured he was totally out of it, but last night I looked it up. It's a really old Native American artifact. I mean *really* old, like four thousand years. It's called a turkey tail because of the way it's shaped."

Roni held the stone in her hand and touched the sharp, scalloped edge. "What did they use it for?"

"Nobody knows for sure. It looks like a spear point, but it's too thin and delicate. The book I read said they were used during ceremonies or as grave furniture."

"Grave furniture?"

"Yeah, like to bury people with. So they can hunt buffalo or whatever in the afterlife."

"Cool."

"Only a few have ever been found in Minnesota. I think it's really rare."

Roni set the artifact carefully on the table. "So the cave might be some sort of tomb? This could be really important! Remember what Eric Bloodwater was telling us on the bus?"

"You mean about his dad owning that land?"

"It's true," Roni said. "My mom filled me in. His dad owns the development company that's going to put up all those ugly condos. Dr. Dart was trying to stop the sale, but he couldn't find any proof that the bluff was an important archaeological site."

"And when he finally found something, he got bonked on the head."

"Do you really think he was attacked?"

"Sure." Brian laughed. "By a ghost."

Roni looked down at the turkey tail. The pale, translucent stone glowed in the evening sun. "This might be just what he needed."

"That, and the skeleton. What do you think we should do? Go to the college? The newspaper?"

"How about your mom? She's a cop."

"She said the police would be talking to Dr. Dart tomorrow, when he got better."

Roni grinned. "Why wait?" she said.

14

family dinner

Eric Bloodwater's mother insisted that Eric and the twins, Sam and Owen, sit down and eat dinner together with her every night. They usually ate on the late side because that was the only way his father could ever join them. Tonight they were having her lasagna, very cheesy and rich, one of Eric's favorite meals.

Often, Mr. Bloodwater didn't even bother to eat with them, even when they had waited for him to get home. He would just pile his plate high and wander off to his upstairs office to make more phone calls. Fred Bloodwater liked to think of himself as a mover and a shaker. He was definitely a mover, Eric thought. They'd moved six times in the past five years.

Eric hoped they would be able to stay put for a while. He liked Bloodwater. Not too small, not too big. A couple of movie theaters, a skateboard park, a good bakery and a decent-size mall. If his father's new development succeeded, he might even be able to finish high school here. Just one more year.

His mom asked him how his class had gone.

"Not bad," he said. "We went for a walk along the Bloodwater River. Kinda boring. But then this really weird thing happened . . ."

Just then his dad walked in and said hi to everyone, giving his wife a kiss on the forehead and mussing the twins' hair. Eric guessed he was too old for his dad to muss his hair anymore.

He smiled inside, thinking about how he was about to blow his dad's mind.

Mr. Bloodwater sat down at the table and said, "Mmm. Lasagna. My favorite." He always claimed everything was his favorite, then wolfed it down like it didn't matter how it tasted.

Eric waited for his dad to finish loading his plate. He could tell his father was about to head upstairs to do some work.

As his father pushed back his chair, Eric said, "Hey, Dad, you hear about what happened at Indian Bluff today?"

His father looked at him. "What are you talking about?"

"A couple of kids found a cave in the bluff."

Mr. Bloodwater frowned. "Cave?"

"Right where the development is going. They went inside and found an old skeleton."

"Cool!" said the twins together.

"Eric, dear, please let's not talk about skeletons at the dinner table," said Mrs. Bloodwater.

Mr. Bloodwater's frown had deepened into a scowl. "I hope that won't hurt our land deal. We're supposed to break ground Friday!"

Eric reached down and scratched at his leg, which had begun to itch. He said, "You'll never guess what else they found in the cave."

Mr. Bloodwater stared at him.

"What?" he finally asked.

"That archaeologist from the college."

"Dart? What was that busybody doing there?"

"I don't know. He was in pretty bad shape when they hauled him out of the cave. I think they took him to Mercy Hospital."

His father stood abruptly and headed toward his office, leaving his astonished wife, his sons and his lasagna behind.

15

colleagues

"I bet I can pop a wheelie in this thing," Brian said. He was sitting in a wheelchair that had been left near the hospital entrance.

"Brian, get out of the wheelchair."

"Push me. I don't feel like walking."

"No."

"Come on. It's a hospital. Wheelchairs are the primary mode of transportation."

Roni was ready to walk away, then decided to call his bluff. "Okay, you want to be transported?" She grabbed the wheelchair and started to push it straight toward the street. Brian came scrambling out of it. Roni stumbled and lost her hold on the wheelchair. The chair continued on its own, bounced over the curb and rolled out onto the street. Before Roni or Brian could retrieve it, an orderly came running out of the hospital and grabbed the chair.

"Don't you kids have anything better to do?" he growled.

"Sorry," Roni said. "It was an accident."

"We're here visiting a friend," Brian added.

"Visit, then. But keep your mitts off the equipment!" He parked the chair and went back inside.

"Good one, Watson," said Roni.

"Hey! I wasn't the pusher."

"Come on—we have work to do."

Dr. Dart's room, they learned, was on the third floor. They took the elevator up.

"I could be relaxing in the deluxe comfort of a wheelchair," Brian pouted.

"You're lucky I don't put you in a wheelchair for real," said Roni. "Turkey trot or no."

"Turkey *tail*," Brian said.

"Here we are." They stopped outside room 313 and looked through the open door. Dr. Andrew Dart was lying in bed staring up at the ceiling.

"Hello? Dr. Dart?"

The archaeologist turned his face toward them.

"Come in! Come in! I've been expecting you!"

Andrew Dart had almost forgotten this meeting with his colleagues. In fact, he couldn't even remember their names, or what they were supposed to be discussing. They looked so young. Perhaps they were graduate students. He hoped they would overlook the fact that he wasn't dressed for the occasion. For some reason he was still in bed. He tried to act composed. He would just have to make do.

At least they had brought in a lovely stone tool for him to identify.

"Very nice," he said, turning it in his hand. "As you can see, it is far too delicate to actually be used for anything. This particular artifact is known as a turkey tail. Where on earth did you come across it?"

"You gave it to me," said the boy.

"I did?" Dart searched his scrambled memory, but encountered only confusion and murk.

"You found it in the cave," said the young woman, who appeared to have a heavy layer of pink makeup on her legs. Young people indulged in such curious fashions these days.

"I'm sorry, what was your name again?" he asked her.

"Roni."

"Yes, of course. Professor Ranee. I must say I'm not sure what you're talking about. This turkey tail appears to be made from Hixton quartzite, which comes from central Wisconsin. I've seen only one like it before, in the collection from the college."

"You found this one in a cave above the Bloodwater River," Professor Ranee insisted. "Don't you remember *anything*?"

Dr. Dart felt the need to lay his head back on the pillow. This meeting wasn't going well at all. They were trying to confuse him.

"Don't you remember the skeleton?"

Skeleton! He had been having horrible dreams of a skeleton trying to chew him up. Rising from a grave. What did it mean? Something important, he was sure, but now he needed to try to get some sleep.

"You said you were attacked," said the younger of the two.

"I was?"

"Yes! In the cave!"

"Cave . . . ?" A memory tugged at his brain. "I remember something . . . I heard footsteps, then something hit me in the head."

"Did you see who it was?"

Dr. Dart closed his eyes, trying to remember. "Yes," he said. "I remember now." He smiled. "It was a ghost!"

The white room began to spin again.

"I really don't feel up to this meeting," he said. "Could we reschedule?"

Just then a square-shouldered woman dressed all in white came into the room. Was she his secretary?

"I think that's just about enough for him today," she said.

"That was a waste of time," said Roni.

"Maybe he'll be better tomorrow."

"We might have to take things into our own hands."

Brian didn't like the sound of that. "What do you mean?"

"Dr. Dart was trying to save the bluff from the developers. If he doesn't get better, we'll have to do it ourselves. He made you swear on the skull, right?"

"He didn't give me a choice. I don't think that counts."

Roni wasn't listening. "I bet he was attacked to keep him from stopping the development."

"My mom said he probably just hit his head on a stalagtite."

"He said he heard footsteps!"

"He also said it was a ghost."

"Well, whether there was an attack or not, the development will wreck a valuable Native American archaeological site, and they're breaking ground this Friday. We have to stop it, or at least delay it until Dr. Dart gets better, so he can complete his investigation."

"How do we stop a bulldozer?"

"With our brains, Einstein. The first thing we do is scope out the enemy. Tomorrow morning Professor Bloom is taking us down to City Hall to watch the developer unveil his ugly condo plans."

"Maybe they won't be as bad as you think," Brian said.

"Maybe they'll be worse."

16

public embarrassment

The next morning, as Brian was just finishing his second bowl of Cap'n Crunch, he heard the putter of Roni's Vespa coming up the street. He shoveled the last few spoonfuls of cereal into his mouth, grabbed his backpack and ran outside.

"Hop on, Watson."

Roni handed him her old pink bike helmet. It was better than nothing.

If his mom saw him on the back of a motor scooter, she'd have a fit, but Brian figured it was worth the risk. Riding to City Hall on a Vespa was ever so much more stylish than walking. And Roni was a pretty good driver. Except when she crashed into things.

The presentation at City Hall was scheduled for 9:00 A.M. Roni and Brian arrived right on time. Roni pulled in between a pickup truck and the school bus, creating her own parking space. Brian admired her creativity. They ran up the steps and went inside, where a receptionist directed them to the meeting. They walked into a large room to find their class sitting near the back. Other than the students, only about two dozen people had shown up for the meeting.

Buddy Berglund, the mayor of Bloodwater, stood on a low stage at the front of the room. He was wearing what

Brian's mom called his "ice-cream suit"—a solid white three-piece suit with wide lapels and flashy gold buttons. The mayor wore his ice-cream suit only for special occasions such as dedicating a new building, swearing in a new police officer or announcing a new trash collection policy.

Charts and maps stood on easels at the front of the room. In big lettering across the top of one chart were the words RIDGEWOOD RESIDENCES. At first Brian was surprised that the name of the condos wasn't Bloodwater something. Maybe Bloodwater wasn't an appealing enough name.

"Today I am honored," Buddy Berglund said, gripping a white lapel with each pudgy pink hand, "*deeply* honored, to introduce to you the great-great-grandnephew of Zebulon Bloodwater, who founded our great city, the man behind Bloodwater Development, Mr. Frederick Augustus Bloodwater!"

The mayor and two or three other people applauded. One of them was Roni's mother, Nick.

Fred Bloodwater, a tall man with a fringe of thin black hair surrounding his shiny dome, loped onto the stage. He wore a dark blue suit with a bright red tie.

"Thank you, thank you," he said, showing off his blindingly white smile. "It is truly an honor to be here today and to have this opportunity to become a part of this fine community . . ."

Blah blah blah. Brian glanced over at Roni, who was staring at Eric Bloodwater. This is not good, Brian thought. Roni's fascination with Eric could only make for problems.

He nudged Roni and pointed at Fred Bloodwater, who was droning on about "quality of life" and "midwestern values."

"That's what Eric is going to look like in twenty years," he said. "No hair."

Roni gave him her you-are-dead-meat look. Brian grinned.

Fred Bloodwater was a fast talker. Brian was trying to follow what he was saying—something about "tax base" and "environmentally friendly" and a bunch of other stuff that didn't sound very sincere—when Roni's voice suddenly cut the air like a knife.

"What about the Indians?" she asked.

Fred Bloodwater stopped talking as if he'd taken a medicine ball to the gut.

"Excuse me?" he said.

"Isn't it true that you're planning to build your condos on an ancient Indian burial ground?" Roni asked.

"I don't . . . No! The area has been fully explored by experts from Bloodwater College. There are no Native American ruins on the property."

"There are according to Dr. Dart," Roni said.

Brian grinned at the flustered expression on Fred Bloodwater's face. Mayor Berglund, standing a few feet to the side, had left his mouth hanging wide open. Brian looked at Roni, who was wearing her glittery-eyed I-gotcha look. A few feet farther on, Eric Bloodwater was smiling at her with open admiration.

And Brian had thought the meeting would be a snore.

Roni felt a familiar hand clamp her upper arm.

"Ow!" she said, even though it didn't really hurt.

"Let's go," her mother whispered in Roni's ear as she lifted her from her seat.

"Okay! Okay!" Nick pushed her out of the room. Behind them, Roni heard someone else ask, "Are there really Indian ruins up there?"

Nick stopped just outside the door and turned on Roni.

"What was that all about?" she demanded.

Roni, rubbing her arm, said, "I was just asking about the burial grounds."

"You can't just blurt things like that out at a public meeting! This development could be very important to Bloodwater. Millions of tax dollars are at stake! In fact, the city of Bloodwater is now a partner in the project—we have invested more than two million dollars in Ridgewood Residences!"

"But Dr. Dart says that the cave could be a major archaeological find!"

"Dr. Dart, from what I've heard, is a raving lunatic."

"Yeah, because somebody bonked him on the head to stop him from investigating. You know, there really is a skeleton in that cave. And he also found this big arrowhead thingy."

"I don't see how that should affect what happens on top of the bluff. And creating a scene at a public meeting is not the way to address this!"

"Isn't that what public meetings are for? To hear what the public has to say?"

"Yes, but—"

"And don't you always tell me not to be afraid to speak my mind?"

"Yes, but . . ."

Roni could see that she had Nick on the run.

"So don't I get to ask a few questions?"

"Yes, but not when it embarrasses me in public!" her mother said. Then she laughed. "I have to admit, though, that look on Buddy's face was almost worth it."

17

epidemic

After the meeting, as Professor Bloom's class gathered outside City Hall, Eric Bloodwater walked up to Roni. At first she thought he was going to say something nasty because she had embarrassed his dad, but Eric leaned in close and said in her ear, "That was so cool!"

A prickly feeling ran up Roni's spine the way it does when somebody you like says something really nice to you.

"Really?" she said, hoping for more.

"Yeah, you totally freaked my dad. I love it!"

"I didn't mean to," Roni said.

Roni looked down and noticed Eric's legs. Like hers, they were covered with red blotches and pink splotches up to his knees.

"I see you've been stricken, too," Roni said.

"Huh?" Eric answered.

"You know, poison ivy." She pointed at her own legs. "It must be an epidemic."

"Oh, wow, you, too? It's driving me crazy."

"Don't scratch," Roni warned him.

"I can't keep my hands off it."

"That just makes it itch more and then it can spread."

"Just so it doesn't spread any higher."

Roni shuddered. She didn't even want to think about

it. For a few seconds they stood in awkward silence. Roni was trying hard to keep her mouth shut about Eric's father's condos. Just because his dad was about to destroy the natural beauty of Indian Bluff didn't mean that Eric was a bad person.

"So ... you really think there's an Indian burial ground?"

"I don't know," Roni said. "But my friend found a—"

"Hey guys!" Brian suddenly popped up between them like a jack-in-the-box.

Brian had a feeling. Usually he wasn't that into feelings and hunches—he preferred facts and figures—but somehow he knew that Eric Bloodwater was bad news. And Roni had been about to tell him about the turkey tail. As far as Brian was concerned, the less Eric Bloodwater knew, the better.

"Hi, Eric," he said, giving him a grin full of braces. He turned to Roni. "Hey, Roni, are you gonna give me a ride home?"

Roni looked flustered. "I don't . . . I guess . . . um . . ."

Brian turned back to Eric. "That didn't go so good for your dad, did it?"

After Roni's mom had escorted her out of the meeting, Fred Bloodwater had been barraged by questions about Indians and burial grounds. The mayor had stepped in and promised that the matter had been "looked into fully and rigorously by authorities," whatever that meant.

Eric shrugged. "He'll be okay. If they won't let him build

on the bluff, he'll build the development down on the bottoms by the river—like he wanted to do in the first place."

"Yeah, but—"

"People! People!" Professor Bloom clapped his hands. "Gather 'round, please. The bus will be leaving in a few minutes. Those of you who arrived by alternate transportation are free to leave at any time."

Brian turned around to say something to Eric and Roni, but Eric had disappeared.

Roni, however, was giving him her dagger look.

"Have I ever told you what a pain in the butt you are?" she asked.

Brian grinned. "Many times."

"I don't see what you've got against Eric," Roni shouted over the whine of the Vespa.

"I don't think we can trust him," Brian yelled in her ear. "You were about to tell him about the turkey tail!"

"So what?"

"So I think we should get solid proof that the cave is an important archaeological site before we let the developer's kid know what we're doing."

Roni pulled up in front of Brian's house.

Brian said, "Who knows? Fred Bloodwater might even be behind the attack on Dr. Dart. Or even Eric."

Roni's eyes narrowed. "So now all of a sudden you think he really was attacked."

"First rule of investigating," Brian said. "Always assume

the worst, and never let on what you know until you have proof in hand."

"That's two rules."

"There are more."

"Okay, okay," Roni said. The kid had a way of wearing her down. "So how do we find this proof?"

"Simple," Brian said as he dismounted. "First thing tomorrow morning, we return to the scene of the crime."

Dinner at the Delicata residence that night was Chinese takeout, which Nick insisted on eating with chopsticks.

"So how did the rest of the meeting go?" Roni asked.

Nick raised one eyebrow, an expression that meant, I can't believe you asked me that. "There were a few tense moments," she said. "But nothing has changed. They'll be breaking ground on Friday."

"They aren't even going to investigate the cave?"

"Eventually, yes. The college will send someone to look things over, and the police are bringing in a forensics expert to look at those old bones. But the development on the bluff is going forward."

"But what about—"

"Roni," Nick interrupted, "I've had a hard day and I really don't want to discuss it."

After cleaning up, Roni went to her room and flopped down on her bed. Why was her mom acting so weird? Usually Nick encouraged her to ask a lot of questions. Roni could hardly believe her mom was in favor of razing

Indian Bluff—Nick was a gung-ho save-the-planet sort of person.

Roni's thoughts were interrupted by a knock on the door. "Come on in."

Nick opened the door and stepped into the room. "I owe you an apology," she said. "I'm sorry I snapped at you."

Roni sat up. She loved it when her mother apologized to her.

"I know you're worried about what will happen to the bluff," Nick said. "I have to tell you, I don't like it, either. But the city has an important stake in this development, and the mayor is very worried that if construction is delayed, it will be a financial disaster for Bloodwater. Fred Bloodwater has convinced the mayor that the town desperately needs this new development, and I'm afraid Buddy isn't about to change his mind."

"Not even if we can prove that Indian Bluff is an important archaeological site?"

"I don't know." Nick shook her head. "You'd need more than one crumbled old skeleton, that's for sure."

"I'll see what I can do," Roni said.

18

blast

"I think you should slow down," Brian shouted.

Roni hated to be told how to drive. She twisted the accelerator and roared through the tall grasses, bushes and weeds that bordered the narrow track leading to the top of the bluff. Brian was clinging on to her backpack. That was her rule for him riding on her Vespa—she didn't want to be seen with his arms around her waist. She liked the kid, but she didn't want anybody to get the wrong idea.

It was early morning. The tall grass was heavy with dew. As they crossed the top of the bluff, they drove past a contractor's storage trailer, with two bulldozers parked nearby. Dozens of wooden surveyor's stakes tied with bits of fluorescent orange ribbon dotted the grassy expanse.

"This is where they're going to build the condos," Roni said.

Brian said, "Slow down! It's right up here!"

Brian was right. The path suddenly opened up, and Roni hit the brakes. They skidded to a stop about three feet from the edge of the bluff.

"That's close enough," said Brian.

Heart pounding, Roni said, "You think so?"

Brian hopped off the scooter and walked up to the brink. The river looked as if it was a mile below them, but he knew it wasn't that far. Looking over the edge, he couldn't see the cave opening, but he could make out the rock ledge just outside the entrance.

"You think we can climb down?" Roni asked.

"Maybe. But not straight down. I think we should try to come at it from a slant. It looks like it might be a little easier from over there." Brian followed the bluff to the left. About twenty yards from where they had parked, the edge of the bluff fell away into a wooded coulee—a steep-sided ravine that sliced into the face of the bluff.

"Maybe we can climb down here, then cut back across to the cave. That way we can make it to the ledge."

Roni said, "Let me know if you see any poison ivy."

"Okay . . . watch your step." Brian climbed down into the coulee, working his way around a tumble of boulders and fallen trees. He was excited to get back to the cave now that he had his trusty flashlight with fresh batteries and his dad's good digital camera so they could record whatever they found. He stopped when he didn't hear any noise behind him. Roni was still standing up on the bluff.

"What's the matter?" Brian asked.

"I don't like coulees. I think maybe we should try to come at it from below, like we did before."

"Are you afraid?" he asked.

"Absolutely not," she said, stepping back from the edge. "I just think a little caution isn't a bad thing."

"You're scared!" Brian couldn't help rubbing it in a little.

Her expression changed and she held up her hand. "Listen."

Brian listened. At first he heard nothing, but then a crunching sound filtered through the trees. Something big was moving through the woods below them, and not far away.

"Probably just a deer," Brian whispered.

"Or a bear," said Roni.

Brian climbed up onto a moss-covered boulder the size of a minivan and peered through the trees. He caught a glimpse of something moving quickly down the coulee. Could be a deer, he thought. But then he saw a flash of red. Deer don't come in red.

"See anything?" Roni asked.

"I saw something red. Maybe a hunter."

"In June?"

"A poacher, maybe."

"I don't think we should go into the woods if . . ." Roni was interrupted by a loud explosion.

Brian would never forget that sound. He had often imagined the world blowing up, and for a moment he thought it might be happening. It sounded like a huge thumb had been jammed inside a really enormous mouth and then come rocketing out with a colossal pop.

A fraction of a second after the explosion, the boulder Brian was standing on shifted, and he came crashing down. He screeched as he fell and then slammed into the earth flat on his back.

After that it seemed very, very quiet. Brian couldn't even hear himself breathe.

Because he wasn't.

Roni's face rose in front of him like a big full moon. She stared down at him. "Are you okay?"

Brian tried to say something, but couldn't. The fall had knocked the wind out of him. He felt as if his lungs had been squeezed flat and glued together. Roni's face grew larger.

"Brian?" Roni's voice rose to a panicky screech.

"Heek, heeek," Brian managed to say—and then Roni was grabbing him, trying to help him sit up. She looks scared, Brian thought as he fought to breathe.

"Brian?" Roni's voice rose another octave.

Brian closed his eyes, and suddenly the bands around his chest loosened and he drew a shuddering breath.

"I . . . I'm okay," he said, even though he wasn't sure it was true. For a few seconds Brian just sat there enjoying the sensation of air flowing in and out of his lungs.

"Are you sure you're okay?" Roni asked.

Brian moved his arms and legs. All in working order. "I'm fine. I think."

"You sure?"

Brian climbed to his feet. He was shaky, but nothing hurt. "Yes . . . except . . ." He reached into the side pocket of his cargo pants and came out with his dad's five-hundred-dollar digital camera—or what was left of it.

"This doesn't look good," Brian said.

"You have to break a few eggs if you want to make lemonade," Roni said. "What was that big bang, anyway?"

Brian remembered what he had seen as the explosion had rocked him from his perch: a fountain of dust and rock erupting from the face of the bluff. "I've got a bad feeling about this."

19

red shirt

Roni followed Brian down the steep coulee as he picked his way around trees and scrambled over boulders.

"Do you think it was our fault? Because we were standing on top of the cave?" Roni asked.

"No way," Brian said. Roni could tell by his tone of voice that Brian thought her concern was stupid. "That was some kind of explosion."

Ten minutes later the coulee spilled out onto a weedy field. They turned right and soon found themselves looking up at the bluff.

"It looks different," Roni said.

"I'm going up," said Brian. He started climbing. Roni stayed behind and watched him make his way up the face of the bluff. It took him only a few minutes to reach the ledge that led to the cave. She waited for him to disappear into the concealed cave entrance, but he just stood there for a few seconds, then came back down the bluff.

"It's gone," he said.

"Gone?"

"No cave. Caveless."

"The cave caved in?" Roni was glad they had not been inside when it happened.

"More like it blew up," Brian said. "Like somebody dynamited the cave entrance."

"Why would someone do that?"

"Obviously to keep anybody from finding out what's inside."

"So now what?" Roni asked, feeling defeated.

"Well, we could get some picks and shovels and start digging . . ."

"Or we could go to the police," said Roni, who did not like the idea of digging her way into a cave full of bats and old bones.

"And tell them what?" Brian said. "Is it illegal to dynamite a cave?"

"I think it's illegal to blow up *anything*. The land belongs to the college. I bet they'd have something to say about it."

"I'm sure Dr. Dart would, if he ever starts—"

"Look!" Roni interrupted, grabbing Brian's sleeve and pointing.

Less than a hundred feet away a young woman was standing in the weeds looking up at the bluff.

"Hey!" Roni shouted.

The woman looked over at them, frowning. Roni started toward her.

Brian, a few steps behind her, said in a low voice, "Notice her T-shirt? It's red!"

"I see it," Roni said.

As they drew closer, Roni raised her voice. "Did you see what happened?"

The woman shook her head. "I heard something." She appeared to be in her late twenties, with a dark tan and long blond hair pulled into a ponytail. She was dressed in khaki shorts and a bright red T-shirt. "It sounded like an explosion."

Roni stopped about ten feet away. Now that she was closer, she could see that the woman was unusually tall and broad shouldered, like a Viking queen.

Roni pulled out her ever-present notebook. "Have you seen anyone else in the area?"

"No. I was walking along the river and I heard the bang, so I came up here to see what it was."

Roni made a note and asked, "And you are . . . ?"

The young woman laughed and her bright eyes glittered like shards of blue ice. "Who are you? The Grand Inquisitor?"

"I'm Roni Delicata," said Roni. "I'm a reporter for the *Bloodwater Pump*."

"I see. Well, if you must know, my name is Jillian Greystone."

20

jillian

Brian thought, Jillian? What had Dr. Dart said about a "Jillian" when they were in the cave? *Don't breathe a word of this to Jillian!*

"What are you doing here?" Brian asked.

Jillian looked at Brian. "What are you, the cub reporter?"

"I'm Brian Bain," said Brian. "Didn't I just see you up in the coulee?"

Jillian Greystone crossed her arms and said, "As I told you, I was down by the river. Now let me ask *you* a question. What are *you* doing here?"

"We came to investigate the cave," said Roni.

"Cave?"

"The cave where I found Dr. Dart," said Brian, pointing up at the bluff.

Fascinated, Brian watched what happened to the woman's face: first her eyes expanded, then her forehead went up and finally her mouth formed a perfect O. Then she managed to say, "You found him?"

Roni said, "Actually, we both found him."

"I found him first," Brian said.

"I had the candle," Roni pointed out.

"I stayed with him."

"I called the ambulance."

"Do you know what happened to him?" Jillian asked.

"Somebody hit him over the head," said Roni.

Jillian frowned. "Are you sure?"

"Yes," said Roni.

"No," said Brian.

Jillian laughed. "That doesn't sound very convincing! The doctors told me he must have tripped and hit his head on a rock. Did he tell you anything about what he was doing in there?"

"He said—ouch!" Roni whirled on Brian, who had just slapped her on the butt. "What was that for?"

"Mosquito," said Brian.

"Did you see anything *interesting* while you were in the cave?" Jillian asked.

Roni said, "There was a—yow! Cut it out!"

"Another mosquito," Brian said. He turned to Jillian. "It was really dark in the cave, and Dr. Dart wasn't making much sense. We came back to take another look inside, but I guess that's out, now that the entrance is sealed up." He gave Jillian a suspicious look. "What do you know about it?"

Jillian shook her head. "Andrew's head injury has him a bit confused," she said. "But I know he was searching the area for Native American artifacts. I wondered whether he had found anything, so I thought I'd survey the area. So far, I haven't seen anything of interest." She looked up at the bluff. "Why would anyone seal off a cave?"

"To keep people out," said Brian. "And by the way, did you know that you're knee deep in a patch of poison ivy?"

21

shock wave

"She seems kind of upset," Brian said as they watched Jillian gallop off toward the river.

"I don't blame her," said Roni, thinking of her own calamine-lotioned legs. "Maybe if she washes up quick, she'll be okay. Fels Naptha is supposed to be the best." She pulled a bar of soap out of her backpack, then tucked it back in. "Now I don't go anywhere without it."

They started walking up to the road.

"I wonder what she—ow!" Brian ducked away from Roni, who had just slapped him on the back of the neck.

"Mosquito," said Roni, lifting one eyebrow. "They seem to be everywhere."

"I just did that so you wouldn't spill the beans!" Brian said.

"What beans? You heard her—she *knows* Dr. Dart. She called him Andrew. And you scared her off. She might be the only person in town who's on our side."

"Yeah, but Dr. Dart warned me about her. He said, 'Don't tell Jillian.' "

"You didn't tell me that."

"I forgot. Who knows, she might be the one who blew up the cave."

"Yeah, right."

"Seriously—she said she was down by the river, but I saw someone wearing red running down the coulee. She could have planted a bomb in the cave, then run back down the coulee to watch it blow up from below."

"But why would she do that?"

"Who knows? Maybe she's a psychotic-likes-to-blow-things-up woman. Or maybe she's secretly working for the developers to keep anybody from finding the skeleton. She might even have been the one who attacked Dr. Dart!"

"I thought you didn't believe he was really attacked."

"I'm keeping my options open. The bottom line is that *somebody* wanted to seal off that cave, and she just happened to be here. That's kind of a huge coincidence, don't you think?"

"*We* just happened to be here, and *we* didn't blow it up," Roni pointed out.

"Yeah, but I don't believe in coincidences. Everything is connected." Brian slapped himself hard on the forehead.

"What?" said Roni. "Did you think of something?"

"No. That was a real mosquito. Let's get out of here."

"Okay. I think it's time for a sugar boost. Something to charge up our brain cells."

"Bratten's or DQ?"

"Your call."

Brian changed his mind about six times on the way downtown. Ice cream or donuts? He wished there was a good place where he could get both. A scoop of chocolate ice cream served on a glazed donut. With sprinkles.

They ended up at Bratten's Café and Bakery, where Roni ordered her usual: three chocolate-glazed French donuts.

"You never get anything else," Brian noted.

"Why attempt to improve upon perfection?" Roni asked as she took a bite from her second French donut.

Brian was working on a bear claw. He had already wolfed down an apple turnover. "So what's the plan, Stan?"

"If you call me Stan again, I'm gonna smoosh this donut in your face."

Brian opened his mouth wide, inviting her to do so.

Roni laughed. "Not a chance, my dear Watson." She finished her donut, then took out her notebook and pen. "The plan is this: we find out who blew up the cave, and what really happened to Dr. Dart, and then we stop the condo development."

Brian was impressed. "You think big," he said.

"If my guess is correct, all three things are connected. Who benefits the most from having that cave sealed off?"

"Bloodwater Development?"

"Exactly! Fred Bloodwater wants his bulldozers to start tearing up Indian Bluff this Friday. If we could have taken some pictures in the cave, the college might have refused to finalize the sale until they investigated the site, and his project would be delayed. Or maybe even canceled."

She wrote in her notebook. Brian, who had trained himself to read upside down, read: *Suspect #1: Fred Bloodwater.*

Roni said, "Fred Bloodwater might also be behind the attack on Dr. Dart."

"Don't forget Jillian Greystone."

"She didn't seem like the mad bomber type."

"What type is that?"

"Well . . . like *you*."

"I never bombed anything!"

"You stink-bombed the school last year!"

"That was an accident!"

Roni laughed and bit into her last donut.

Brian said, "Anyway, I think we should check her out. She could be secretly working for the developers. Until we find out differently, she should go on the list of suspects."

Roni brushed donut crumbs from her notebook and wrote down *Jillian Greystone.* "Who else?" she asked, pen poised.

"Eric Bloodwater," Brian said.

"Eric?" Roni's voice rose three octaves. "Why?"

"Because he knows where the cave is, and he's his father's son. And don't forget, during the field trip he ditched Gennifer and disappeared. He could have attacked Dr. Dart, too. Also, he's a Bloodwater, if you know what I mean."

"You're prejudiced against Bloodwaters?"

"Everybody knows all the Bloodwaters were nuts. Like the last ones to live there. Crazy Farley Bloodwater tried to kill his brother Zeb, then disappeared, and then Zeb built a pair of wings and tried to fly off Barn Bluff. My dad knew them, you know."

"He did?"

"He was their newspaper boy. They still owe him two dollars."

"What's that got to do with Eric?" Roni asked.

Brian sighed. Most of the time Roni was one of the smartest people he knew, but when it came to good-looking boys, she could be as dense as lead.

"Look, I know you're in love with him, but that doesn't—"

"I am NOT in love with him," Roni interrupted, squinting her eyes dangerously.

"Whatever, I just think we should keep an eye on him."

Roni said, "I'm sure he didn't—"

"What is with you?" Brian interrupted. "I thought you were a turn-over-every-stone-to-uncover-the-truth investigative reporter. Just because you like Eric doesn't mean we can't investigate him!"

Roni sat back. For a few seconds, Brian thought she was going to launch herself across the table and strangle him, but slowly her expression changed. She shrugged and gave him a half smile.

"You're right," she said, adding Eric's name to the list.

Brian practically fell off his chair. He was right? Roni Delicata was telling him he was right? Was he dreaming?

"Are you okay?" he asked.

"That explosion concussed me, I think."

"I'm the one who fell off the rock."

"I was closer to the shock wave."

"That would be a good name for a band—Shock Wave."

82

"Back to the digging, Watson." She tapped her notebook. "We should try to talk to Professor Dart again. And investigate the Bloodwaters. And find out who Jillian Greystone is."

Brian looked at his watch. "Class doesn't start for another couple of hours. Let's go to the hospital and see if Dr. Dart is making any sense today."

Roni said, "I've got a better idea. Why don't *you* go see Dr. Dart, and *I'll* investigate the Bloodwaters."

Seeing the expression on her face Brian thought, Uh-oh.

22

samowen

Riding up Riverview Terrace on Hillary, Roni was relieved not to have Brian Bain clinging to her backpack. Much as she liked him, the kid could be a real pain in the butt. All that stuff about her being in love with Eric Bloodwater . . . ridiculous!

Let Brian listen to Dr. Dart's senseless babbling. Roni would go straight to the heart of the matter. She pulled over to the curb and looked up at the mansion known as Bloodwater House.

Bloodwater House was the biggest home in Bloodwater, and one of the oldest. It had been built in the 1890s by James J. Bloodwater, the son of Zebulon J. Bloodwater, who had founded the town back in 1867. Built entirely of native limestone, Bloodwater House had four enormous pillars on either side of the front door. There were more than thirty rooms inside. The house was completely surrounded by a ten-foot-tall wrought iron fence. Each vertical bar was topped by a large iron spear point.

Roni shuddered. Bloodwater House held some very scary memories for her. It was there that she and Brian had solved the mystery of the Alicia Camden kidnapping. Alicia and her parents were gone now, but the sight of the house still sent a chill up her spine. Everyone who had ever lived there had come to a bad end, and now, for the first time in half a century, the home was once again occupied by Bloodwaters.

Roni walked up to the front gate and rang the bell. A few seconds later the front door opened and two identical black-haired heads looked out at her, blinking blue eyes. The two boys stared at her for several heartbeats, then pushed the heavy door all the way open and ran down the walk to the gate.

"Who are you?" they asked with one voice.

Roni smiled down at the two boys, obviously twins. "My name's Roni," she said. "Is Eric home?"

"Eric is our brother," said one of the twins. They looked to be about seven years old.

"I thought so," said Roni. "What are your names?"

"SamOwen," said the twins. She couldn't tell which boy had said which name.

"Okay, SamOwen, is your brother home?"

One of the twins unlatched the gate, and both of them tore back down the walk to the house and disappeared inside, leaving the door open. Roni walked up to the house and looked in through the door. The twins had disappeared.

She stepped into the cavernous marble foyer. The house smelled like moist stone and old dust. "Hello?" she said.

"Bet you can't find us!" A voice echoed down the hall.

Kids, Roni thought. Brian would fit right in here.

She crossed the foyer and entered a long hallway. Most of the doors lining the hall were open.

"Hello?" she called out. Her voice sounded small. She moved deeper into the house, peeking into each doorway as she passed. Most of the rooms were empty—not even a stick of furniture. She supposed that it would cost a fortune to furnish a house of this size.

She raised her voice. "Eric!"

She heard laughter that seemed to come from inside the walls.

Roni continued through the house and eventually reached a large room with windows from floor to ceiling. Several dozen potted plants were clustered near the windows, which overlooked the five-sided swimming pool in the backyard. Roni had once fallen into that pool. She shivered, remembering the cold water closing over her head. But now the pool was dry, its sides green with dry algae.

"Hey."

Roni whirled, startled by the voice. It was Eric.

"How'd you get in?" Eric asked. He was dressed in baggy shorts and a red tank top. His hair was tousled and off-center, as if he'd just awakened from a nap.

"Your brothers let me in," Roni said.

"They're not supposed to do that," Eric said.

"Oh. Sorry. I didn't know. Are you babysitting?"

"Not really. My mom's upstairs taking a nap. What are you doing here?"

"I . . . um . . ." Roni realized that she hadn't quite thought out a good excuse for her visit. "I'm writing an article on

Bloodwater House. You know, about how the Bloodwater family is taking over the old homestead?"

"Oh. Cool. You should probably talk to my dad. He's all interested in history and stuff. But he's not home."

"Actually I was hoping I could talk to you. Get the youth perspective."

"Oh." Eric shrugged. "It's like living in an airplane hangar. I mean, these ceilings are thirty feet high. We have birds in the house."

Right on cue, a chittering sparrow flew over their heads and landed on one of the plants.

"Have you ever been in here before?" Eric asked.

"Just once," Roni said. "I got lost."

"Yeah, that can happen here. You want a tour?"

"Sure."

As Eric walked her through the house, Roni asked him questions about the architecture and about Bloodwater family history. He didn't seem to know much, so she decided to enlighten him.

"Hasn't anybody told you about the Bloodwater Curse?" she asked.

Eric gave her a confused look.

"What curse?"

"The Bloodwaters who lived here before had some pretty bad luck. Like the guy who built the house, James J. Bloodwater. He was trimming his rosebushes one day and got struck by lightning. And back in the 1960s Farley

Bloodwater—Crazy Farley—went insane and tried to kill his brother right there in Bloodwater House."

Eric's jaw dropped.

"Why did he do that?"

"The story is that a chandelier fell on Farley. Right here in the dining room. It cracked his skull wide open. The doctors were able to repair his skull, but as soon as he got out of the hospital, Farley came back here and tried to kill his brother, who he accused of loosening the chandelier. Farley was charged with attempted murder. Then, during the trial, he grabbed a gun from the bailiff, shot his own lawyer and ran out of the courthouse and into the woods. They never caught him."

"Maybe he's still out there," said Eric.

"He'd be pretty old by now. But that's not all. A few years later his brother built a set of wings out of balsa wood and silk and launched himself off Barn Bluff. He didn't survive. And a woman who lived here hanged herself from the fence."

Eric shrugged. "Well, I'm not gonna be doing any flying or hanging. And we don't have any chandeliers. Come on—I want to show you my dad's office."

On the way upstairs, Roni could hear the twins laughing, but she couldn't tell where it was coming from.

"Owen and Sam are playing hide-and-seek," Eric explained. "They do that all the time."

Eric was showing her his father's oversize oak-paneled office when Roni brought the conversation around to the development.

"So is your dad going ahead with the development?" she asked.

"Of course. That's what we came here for."

"Where did you live before?"

"We've lived all over—Texas, Colorado, California. My dad does all kinds of real estate deals."

"So why did he have to come all the way back here to tear up Indian Bluff?"

Eric laughed. "My dad doesn't care about that Indian stuff. Besides—" He hesitated. "How come *you* care about it so much?"

"I just don't think you should destroy artifacts that have been preserved for thousands of years."

"What artifacts? That archaeologist just has it in for us. My dad says that if archaeologists had their way, we'd never build anything at all."

"I thought you liked it when I brought it up at the meeting yesterday."

"I thought it was cool that you tweaked the old man in public, but that doesn't mean I want his big project to fail. He's spent months on this deal."

"So the bulldozers are going to just tear up the bluff?" Roni felt herself starting to lose it.

Eric laughed. "Bulldozers, trenchers, dynamite, whatever it takes. So what?"

She wanted to punch him. "So they could wait a few days to give Dr. Dart a chance to recover and investigate the cave!"

"Cave? I heard there was some sort of cave-in."

"Where'd you hear that?" Roni asked. It had been only a couple of hours since she and Brian had witnessed the explosion. How could Eric have gotten the news so quickly?

"One of my dad's construction engineers went out there. He told us."

"Yeah, right. I bet your dad wrecked the cave himself."

Eric threw back his head and laughed. "My dad? He's so scared of dynamite he won't go within a mile of the stuff."

Roni felt herself go all cold inside. "How did you know the cave was dynamited?" she asked.

"How else would you cave-in a cave?"

Roni didn't know what to say. Then Eric surprised her.

"You're kind of different, aren't you?"

"What do you mean?" said Roni, cautiously pleased that he was noticing anything at all about her.

"I mean, you're into saving the dead Indians. And I heard you got involved in some kidnapping a while ago."

Roni shrugged modestly. "I like to check things out," she said.

"You're, like, Mystery Adventure Girl. You went into that cave the other day. You like dark spooky places? Hey, you want to see something really cool?"

"Sure, but don't we have to get going pretty quick? We have to go to class pretty soon."

"This won't take long," Eric said. He stepped over to the oak-paneled wall and ran his fingers along the seam between two of the heavy panels. Roni heard a click, and the panel slid aside to reveal a hidden doorway about four feet high.

"I found this one day when we were cleaning," he said.

Roni looked inside. The opening led to a dark, dusty, narrow passageway.

"Check it out," he said.

Curious, Roni ducked her head and entered the passageway. She became immediately uncomfortable—it reminded her too much of the cave. She started to back out when she heard the click of the panel closing behind her.

23

thirteen steps

The scariest thing about visiting people in hospitals, Brian thought, was that the person might be dead. This had happened to him once when he had gone to visit his grandmother. He had known that she had cancer and didn't have long to live, but that didn't make it any less horrible when he stopped by Mercy Hospital to find her room empty. He had then found his mother sitting in the waiting room, crying, with his dad's arm around her.

Brian felt that little tingle of fear in his belly as he waited for the elevator, even though he didn't know Dr. Dart that well. You just never knew.

The elevator doors opened and out stepped Professor Bloom.

"Bain!" The professor stopped in surprise.

"Hi, Professor," said Brian.

"What are you doing here?" asked Professor Bloom.

"I came to see how Dr. Dart is doing."

"I see. I was just visiting him myself. The poor man seems to be a bit addled."

"I was hoping he'd be better today."

"I fear that is not the case." The professor looked at his watch. "Don't forget, you are due in class in one hour. The unfortunate Dr. Dart was supposed to visit our class today, but I have instead arranged for one of his associates to be on hand. Do not be late." He thumped the rubber tip of his cane on the floor for emphasis.

"I'll be there," Brian said.

The professor stalked off quickly with his cane held like a rifle over his shoulder. Brian stepped into the elevator and pressed the button for the third floor. When the elevator doors opened, Brian nearly collided with a tall, fast-moving blond woman. Brian turned to look at the woman as she got into the elevator. It was Jillian Greystone. Their eyes locked in mutual astonishment as the elevator doors slid closed.

First Professor Bloom, then Jillian Greystone. That was a weird coincidence, Brian thought.

And then he remembered that he didn't believe in coincidences.

At first, Roni wasn't scared. Eric had to be just joking around. The panel would open any second and he would laugh and she would get mad and . . . what was he waiting for? Five seconds was maybe a little funny. Fifteen seconds in utter darkness was un-funny.

"Hey!" she yelled, banging her fist on the panel. It felt as solid as the trunk of an oak. "Cut it out, Eric! Not funny!"

She listened, but heard no response.

Fifteen seconds was un-funny; thirty seconds was verging on scary. She felt along the edges of the panel but could find no knobs, levers or hidden catches.

Sixty seconds was even scarier than thirty seconds. Roni could feel her heart pounding.

"LET ME OUT!" she shouted. She braced herself against the opposite wall and kicked the panel as hard as she could. All she managed to do was stir up dust and practically break her foot.

She wished she had her scented candle, but she had left her backpack in the front hallway.

Coughing and limping, Roni worked her way along the narrow passageway. It had to lead someplace. She moved slowly, sliding one foot forward at a time, feeling along the walls with her hands. She imagined Eric standing outside in the hall, laughing. What did he think he was doing? Fear gave way to anger, and with each sliding step Roni swore that when she got out of there, she would kill Eric Blood-water. No, killing was too easy. She would imprison him in an underground tomb with nothing but liverwurst and asparagus to eat. She would—

Roni let out a yelp as her right foot met nothingness. She flailed about with her arms, searching for something to grab onto, but she couldn't stop herself from falling forward into the dark.

Brian walked down the hall to room 313 and peeked inside. Dr. Dart was sitting up in bed talking to a dark-skinned man with a bandage wrapped around his head. At first Brian thought the dark-skinned man was another patient, but then he realized that it wasn't a bandage on the man's head—it was a turban.

"I'm not a ghost, Dr. Dart. I'm a Sikh," the man said.

"I don't care how sick you are," said Dr. Dart.

"I'm not 'sick,' " the man said, laughing. "You're the one who's sick. I'm a *Sikh*. This is our traditional head-wear."

"Where are you from?"

"I'm Indian."

"Indian? Last time I saw you, you were dead!"

"I'm not dead, Dr. Dart," said the man. "I'm your doctor. Doctor Singh."

Brian stepped into the room. "Hi," he said.

Dr. Singh turned and said, "Can I help you?"

"I just came to visit Dr. Dart," Brian said. "How is he?"

"He's had quite a blow to the head," said Dr. Singh.

"Stop spinning like that," said Dr. Dart.

"So you think somebody hit him on the head?"

"At first we assumed that he had fallen and hit his head on a rock," said Dr. Singh. "But when I reexamined his wound, I noticed that it had very smooth edges, almost as if he'd been hit with a pipe, or a heavy rod of some sort. A rock would have left a more jagged wound."

"It was a ghost," offered Dr. Dart.

Dr. Singh smiled, but his forehead wrinkled with concern. "Just try to relax, Dr. Dart. I'll be back to check on you shortly." Dr. Singh left the room.

Brian approached the bedside. "Hi, Dr. Dart. Do you remember me?"

Dr. Dart focused his eyes on Brian. "Yorick? Is that you?"

"It's Brian Bain," said Brian.

"Dr. Brain! Have you seen Yorick?"

"Um, not lately. Dr. Dart, you know Jillian Greystone?"

"Jillian?" He looked around wildly.

"Who exactly is she, Dr. Dart?

Dr. Dart's eyes welled with tears. He said, "She'll never forgive me, you know. I love her, but she hates me!"

"Why? What did you do?"

Dr. Dart looked away, and for a moment Brian thought he saw a glint of sanity in his eyes. "I forgot she was a human," he said. "I forgot she had feelings."

"Do you remember anything more about what happened to you?"

Dr. Dart put his index finger in his mouth, digging between his teeth. He pulled his finger out of his mouth and looked at it.

"They put rocks in your mouth when you're sleeping," he said, showing Brian a tiny, dark oblong shape, smaller than a peppercorn, stuck to the tip of his finger.

Roni landed hard, scraping her knee on the floor and banging her head on the wall. She lay there for a few seconds wondering if she was mortally injured. Except for the pain in her knee and head, she seemed to be okay. She sat up and felt around, trying to figure out what had happened. She felt a step, and another, and another, and another. She had fallen down four steps onto a landing.

Groping around in the dark, she found another set of steps leading down. Counting, she carefully descended the next staircase. Thirteen steps. Good thing she hadn't fallen down that one.

The passageway went off in two directions at the bottom of the steps. Roni flipped a mental coin and turned to the left. Sooner or later, she told herself, I'm going to get out of here. But another part of her remembered reading that one resident of Bloodwater House—Crazy Farley—had disappeared, never to be found. She imagined herself stumbling across his body. Somehow, once she thought of it, she couldn't think about anything else. What would it feel like to step on a dried-up dead person? What kind of crunch would it make?

Just as she was having that unpleasant thought, someone shrieked in her ear and she was blinded by a brilliant flash of light.

Roni screamed and ran straight into a wall.

"GotchaGotcha!" squealed two identical voices.

Brian found Dr. Singh standing at the nurses' station.

"Dr. Singh?"

"Yes? Oh, Dr. Dart's young friend."

"What's wrong with him?" Brian asked. "Why isn't he getting better?"

Dr. Singh frowned and his turbaned head bobbed on his thin neck. "Head wounds can produce unpredictable effects," he said. "But I've never seen a case quite like Dr. Dart. This morning, with his other visitors, he was quite lucid. He was talking about going back to that cave where he was injured. Something about some Native American artifacts. He is very passionate about his work!"

"He's kinda out of it right now," Brian said.

Dr. Singh did his bobblehead thing again and said, "Yes, he seems to be experiencing both auditory and visual hallucinations, almost as if he were drugged."

"He says somebody has been putting rocks in his mouth," said Brian. He held out his hand. In the center of his palm was the tiny black seedlike object Dr. Dart had picked from between his teeth. "Why would he have rocks in his mouth?"

"That was *not* funny!" Roni said, touching the fresh bump on her forehead.

Sam and Owen giggled. They were all standing in the narrow passageway, now illuminated by a bare bulb hanging from the ceiling. Roni could see that there was a bulb hanging every ten feet or so, each with a pull-cord switch hanging just above head level. If she had known they were there, she could have turned them on at any time.

"It's not nice to scare people," Roni said.

"But it's *funny*," said Owen. Or Sam.

"How does your mom tell you apart?" Roni asked.

"She calls us both SamOwen," said SamOwen.

"Sometimes she calls us OwenSam," said OwenSam.

"Your big brother is an ass," Roni said.

"She said ASS!" squealed SamOwen. The twins collapsed in a giggling fit.

Roni waited for the hilarity to subside, then said, "I just meant he isn't very nice to have locked me in here."

"He locked us in here once, too," said one of the twins. "Only we figured out how to escape. Now we have a special name for him. Do you want to hear it?"

"Uh, sure," said Roni.

"POOPHEAD!" shrieked the twins.

Roni laughed. "Good name," she said.

"We have other names, too. Do you want to know what Poophead's secret name is?"

Roni braced herself for another shriek.

"Fenton," said SamOwen.

"Fenton?"

"Yes. We all have secret names. My secret name is Tyler, and his is Preston."

Roni smiled. When she was their age, she'd had a secret name, too. She'd called herself Zenoba, Queen of Glymmerland.

"You want to know what our dad's secret name is? It's Fitzroy!" said the twin on the left.

"And our mom's secret name is Camillia," said the other.

"Now your secret names aren't secret anymore," Roni said.

"You won't tell anybody, will you?"

"Your secrets are safe with me. Now, how do we get out of here?" she asked.

"You can get out lots of ways," said SamOwen.

"How about the closest way?"

One of the twins ran a few yards down the passage and slid open a panel similar to the one by which she had entered. Roni quickly followed and found herself standing in the front foyer.

"Now," she said, "where's your brother?"

"He's gone," said Sam. Or Owen.

"Gone where?"

"I think he went to school."

24

old bones

On the way to the school Roni stopped at the Quik Mart and bought a megasize grape slushy. It was a little tricky transporting it on her Vespa. She had to hold it between her legs as she drove. By the time she got to the school, her thighs were practically frostbitten, but she hadn't spilled a drop. Carrying her backpack in one hand and the slushy in the other, she walked in and scanned the classroom for Eric Bloodwater. It took her a second to find him slumped in a desk near the back of the room. Without hesitating, Roni walked up behind him.

"Hey, Poophead," she said.

Eric looked around, startled, as Roni popped the plastic lid off the slushy and poured it over his black curls.

Eric let out a yelp and jumped straight up out of his seat.

Roni turned her back and went to the far side of the room and sat down, her face burning. Everybody in the room was staring at her. She didn't care.

Purple and completely soaked, Eric stalked out of the classroom, nearly colliding with a startled Professor Bloom in the doorway.

Brian, sitting at the next desk, leaned over to Roni and asked her, "How did it go?"

"Shut up," Roni said, not looking at him.

A few rows over, Gennifer Kohlstad and Franny Hall were talking and giggling and looking at her, no doubt enjoying the fact that this beautiful summer day they were forced to spend in Dullsville had been interrupted by a moment of drama.

Professor Bloom, checking his watch, looked over the rest of the class and nodded. "With the exception of Mr. Bloodwater, we all seem to be here," he said. "As you may know, Dr. Andrew Dart was supposed to be here today to discuss the archaeology of Bloodwater Locality." He cleared his throat. "However, because of his unfortunate accident, Dr. Dart will not be able to join us. Instead, we are fortunate to have one of Dr. Dart's illustrious colleagues—" He nodded toward the back of the room.

Roni turned to see who he was looking at.

"—Miss Jillian Greystone."

Jillian Greystone had changed her clothes since Brian had last seen her. She was now dressed in ragged jeans with dirt ground into the knees, and a rather dirty and sun-faded chambray shirt with the sleeves rolled up. Several turquoise-and-silver bracelets hung from her wrists. On her head was a floppy, wide-brimmed canvas hat with a feather jutting jauntily from the band, and over her shoulder hung a beat-up leather satchel.

Brian thought she looked great—like a warrior woman in denim and turquoise. And he was relieved to find out that she worked with Dr. Dart. Maybe she wasn't the mad bomber after all.

On the other hand, Dr. Dart had said that she hated him. Maybe they were professional rivals.

He had brought the turkey tail with him, hoping to show it to the anthropologist from the college—but he hadn't known that the anthropologist would be Jillian Greystone.

"Thank you, Professor," said Jillian Greystone as she strode toward the front of the room in her battered Red Wing boots. Professor Bloom got up from his desk and offered her his chair. Jillian Greystone, a good two inches taller than the professor, shook her head. Instead, she plunked down her satchel, sat down on top of his desk, then drew up her long legs and crossed them Indian-style.

Professor Bloom started to say something, changed his mind and withdrew to the side of the room, scowling. Jillian Greystone ignored him. She propped her elbows on her knees and looked over the class. Her eyes stopped on Roni and Brian, and her face did the same thing it had done back at Indian Bluff: her eyes went big, her forehead rose and her mouth formed an O.

Brian waggled his fingers at her.

Jillian Greystone's expression returned to neutral and she looked over the rest of the class. Satisfied, she cleared her throat and spoke.

"My name, as Professor Bloom mentioned, is Jillian Greystone. Please call me Jillian. Now, what do you think of when you hear the word *archaeologist*?"

Nobody said anything for a few seconds. Then Gennifer Kohlstad raised her hand and said, "Old bones."

"Old bones," repeated Jillian. "Very good. What else?"

"Indiana Jones," said Brianna Wipsted.

"T. rex!" shouted Liam Dressler, a sixth-grader.

Brian liked Liam. It was good to have someone smaller and more immature in the class. Took the pressure off.

"Very good," said Jillian, "although Indiana Jones is more of a grave robber than an archaeologist. As for the dinosaurs, that is a specialized branch of archaeology known as paleo-archaeology. But today I'm going to talk about a very specific area of archaeology—the study of graves, buildings, tools and pottery from past human cultures here in the Bloodwater Locality. Oh, by the way"— she smiled and spread her arms—"I wore my working clothes today so you could see what a real archaeologist looks like. We spend a lot of time on our hands and knees digging in the dirt. Now, I'd like to begin by talking about the Native American peoples who lived in the Bloodwater Locality about one thousand years ago . . ."

Jillian Greystone was big, beautiful, confident and smart—everything Roni admired in a woman. But that didn't make her any less boring. Five minutes into the lecture Roni's attention began to fade.

". . . from approximately nine hundred A.D. up into the

thirteen hundreds, the Native American peoples in this area . . .

". . . influences from the Woodland peoples, the Oneota peoples and the Mississippians, an advanced culture centered in Cahokia, five hundred miles to the south . . .

". . . artifactual evidence gathered at the Silvernale and Hamlin sites offers a distinctive . . ."

Soon Roni was watching Jillian's mouth moving, but the words had ceased to penetrate. She looked around at the other students. Only Brian seemed to be listening. Everybody else, including Professor Bloom, looked as if they were slipping into a coma.

". . . the Altithermal period significantly affected previously grendalboffer wisthammers, and undleratherflxzbff—"

Roni was fading fast. The situation called for desperate measures. She raised her hand.

"Yes?" said Jillian.

Roni scrambled for a question. "Umm . . . what about Indian Bluff? Aren't they about to build condos on an important archaeological site?"

"I don't believe so," said Jillian. "Despite its name, Indian Bluff shows no evidence that it was ever occupied by Native Americans."

"Not according to Dr. Dart," Roni said.

Jillian blinked and took a moment before answering.

"Dr. Dart is mistaken," she said. "I visited the bluff this morning, as you well know, and saw nothing of interest—other than a rather large patch of toxic vegetation. The bulldozers will be breaking ground on Friday, and without solid evidence of Native American habitation there's nothing anyone can do about it."

"But—"

"I think that rather than explore Andrew Dart's unproven theories, we should concentrate on what we do know. Now, as I was saying, precontact cultures in the Bloodwater Locality left considerable artifactual evidence, including—"

She frowned and looked at Brian.

"Young man, what is that you have in your hands?"

25

bods

"Nothing!" Brian quickly put the turkey tail back in his pocket. He had taken it out because it was poking him in the leg, and Jillian had caught sight of it.

She uncrossed her long legs and walked up to his desk.

"Let me see."

Brian handed her the turkey tail.

Jillian returned to her perch on the desk and examined the stone. "It's beautiful," she said. "A nearly perfect specimen. Wherever did you get it?"

"Dr. Dart gave it to me," Brian said. "In the cave."

"Why would he bring an artifact such as this into the cave?"

"That's where he found it," Brian said.

Jillian shook her head. "Unlikely. This type of point is extremely rare in our area, and quartzite does not occur in the Bloodwater Locality. I suspect that Andrew—Dr. Dart—borrowed the item from our collection at the college, though why he would . . . oh, dear. You don't suppose . . . no, Andrew would never do such a thing."

"Such a thing as what?" Brian asked.

Roni thought she knew what Jillian was thinking. "You think that Dr. Dart was planning to plant the turkey tail in the cave?"

Jillian seemed to forget that she was standing in front of a classroom full of students.

"Andrew was very upset about the development," she said. "He was at the point where he would do anything to stop it—even blow off his own engagement party. He might even plant false archaeological evidence. I wouldn't put it past him."

"Yeah, but would he have hauled an entire skeleton into the cave?" Roni asked.

"Skeleton?"

"A *human* skeleton," Brian said.

"This is the first I've heard about any skeleton. Are you certain?"

"Yeah. It had a skull and everything. Dr. Dart called it Yorick."

"Yorick? I guess you must be telling me the truth. Andrew called all his bods Yorick. It's from *Hamlet*."

"What is 'his bods'?" asked Brian.

"Dead people. More properly, human remains. Some field anthropologists call them bods. Andrew always addressed his bods as Yorick. Andrew was a little strange even before he got bonked on the head."

Roni asked, "What's your relationship with Dr. Dart? Do you just work together?"

Jillian suddenly realized that twenty sets of eyes were on her.

"We are not here to discuss my personal life," she said.

"I'm an investigative reporter. Reporters ask questions."

"You may ask me your questions after class." She set the turkey tail on the desk. "Now, as I was saying, artifacts left by precontact cultures are . . ."

Roni and Brian stayed behind after class to talk to Jillian.

"So what's the deal with you and Dr. Dart?" Roni asked, going right to the heart of the matter.

"As you know, Andrew and I both teach archaeology at the college, and we have worked together on research projects."

"Are you friends?"

Jillian's smile flattened. "I would not say that, no."

"Rivals?"

Jillian lowered her eyes and did not answer right away. Then she shrugged. "I guess it's no secret—everybody at the college certainly knows. Until a few days ago, Andrew and I were engaged to be married. Until he decided that dead people mattered to him more than the living."

Roni waited for details, but Jillian had gone back to examining the turkey tail.

"It's not like Andrew to be giving away valuable artifacts," Jillian said. "On my last birthday he gave me a set of plastic coffee mugs. Even my engagement ring was a fake diamond. He would never give away an artifact this valuable."

Brian said, "I don't think he was actually giving it to me to keep. I think he wanted me to take care of it." He reached out to take the stone back, but Jillian held it out of his reach.

"I believe Andrew borrowed this from the college's collection. I'll see that it's returned." She put the turkey tail in her shirt pocket. "I have to be going now."

"But . . . what about Yorick?" Brian said.

"And the development?" Roni added.

Jillian shook her head. "Indian Bluff was Andrew's obsession. If it weren't for Indian Bluff, we would be married now. As far as I'm concerned, the bulldozers can have it."

"But what if it really is an important archaeological find? The cave could be full of important artifacts."

"I very much doubt that." Jillian smiled with her mouth, but her eyes were expressionless.

Brian said, "Hey, can I look at the turkey tail again?"

Jillian frowned, then took the turkey tail from her pocket and held it out. Brian snatched the artifact from her hand and took off running.

Jillian shouted, "Hey!" She stared after Brian, open-mouthed, as he ran out the door.

"He . . . he can't do that!" she said after a moment.

"He just did," said Roni, both shocked and proud of Brian's act. "He's very attached to his turkey tail."

Outside the school Roni looked around for Brian, but he was gone. She shook her head. That kid always managed to surprise her. She climbed onto Hillary and was pulling her helmet over her head when Eric Bloodwater walked up to her.

"Hey," he said.

Roni narrowed her eyes. "Hey yourself, Poophead."

Eric laughed. "I guess you got me good," he said, looking down at his purple-stained shirt and shorts.

"Less than you deserved," said Roni. "Locking me in that passage."

Eric shrugged. "I'm sorry," he said, not looking at all sorry. "I thought . . . you know . . . you're Adventure Girl! I thought you'd think it was fun!"

"I think you just wanted to scare the crap out of me. Not funny. Not fun."

"Oh." He looked confused. "Well, anyways, we're even now. So . . . you want to grab a coffee or something?" He grinned.

Roni looked at his white smile, at his ever-so-slightly-crooked teeth. She looked at the sheen of dried grape slushy still on his neck, and she looked into his amazing blue eyes.

And then she thought about how angry and scared and betrayed she had felt when he locked her in the secret passage. Why did boys have to be so incredibly boneheaded?

"Tell you what," he said. "Since you spilled your other one, how about I buy you a grape slushy."

So incredibly cute and charming and irresistible?

26

slushy date

"Hey, Dad." Brian, standing in the doorway to his father's office, waited for a response. So many books were piled on Bruce Bain's desk that he couldn't tell if anybody was back there. He raised his voice. "Dad?"

No answer. Brian eased into the office, squeezing between piles of document boxes and file cabinets, and checked behind his father's desk. No Bruce Bain.

That was odd. His father rarely left his office during the day.

Brian went through the rest of the house. He checked his parents' bedroom, the kitchen, the back porch and the basement. No dad.

Expanding his search to the outside, Brian finally found his father behind the house standing on the top rung of a stepladder staring intently at the underside of the eave.

Brian waited, not saying anything. Bruce Bain, when concentrating, had a habit of jumping out of his skin when startled. Brian didn't want to make his dad fall off the ladder, so he stood quietly and waited for him to finish doing whatever he was doing. After a few minutes a black, long-legged wasp dropped from between the eave and the gutter and flew off. Bruce Bain lowered his head, blinking rapidly, and climbed down the ladder. Brian waited until he had reached the safety of solid ground before speaking.

"Hey, Dad."

Bruce Bain jumped, but only a little. "Brian!" he said, as if it were the most remarkable thing in the world that he would encounter his own son in his own backyard.

"What were you looking at?" Brian asked.

"I was observing the nest-building behavior of *Sceliphron caementarium*."

"Oh. What's that?"

"The black-and-yellow mud dauber."

"Oh. What's *that*?"

"A species of solitary wasp." Bruce Bain pointed up at the eave. "She's building a nest of mud. Quite fascinating, actually."

"Aren't you afraid you'll get stung?"

Bruce Bain looked puzzled. "That had not occurred to me."

"Dad, if somebody gives you something, and then you show it to somebody, and they say, 'Hey, that doesn't belong to you,' and they take it, and then you grab it back and run away, can you be arrested?"

Bruce Bain touched his finger to his chin and thought.

"That would depend . . . ," he said.

Brian groaned internally. He hated answers that start out with "That would depend . . ."

". . . upon the legal ownership of the object in question, the laws of the nation in which the event occurred, the in-

113

tentions of the parties in question, the knowledge possessed at the time of the confiscation by each party and the nature of the object itself. If, for example, the object were a child, and the parties in question were its parents, then the situation would become far more complex than if they had been fighting over, say, a dishrag."

"Why would anybody fight over a dishrag?"

"I can think of several possible scenarios—"

"That's okay, Dad. I get it." Brian backed away, hoping to escape before it occurred to his dad to load him up with a stack of law books. He pointed up at the eave. "I think your mud dauber is back."

"Excellent. Say, have you seen my camera?"

"Umm . . . not lately, Dad." Brian ducked into the house and ran up to his room, feeling awful. Sooner or later he would have to own up to destroying his father's camera, but now wasn't the time. He traced his fingers along the sharp edges of the turkey tail. Had Dr. Dart really stolen it from the artifact collection at the college? He didn't believe it. Jillian Greystone had to be mistaken. Or lying.

He hoped he hadn't gotten himself in trouble again. If the turkey tail really was the property of the college, he might wind up being arrested by his own mother.

He wondered what Roni thought about his running off with the turkey tail. He picked up the phone and dialed her number. The answering machine picked up after four rings. Instead of leaving a message, Brian hung up, turned to his computer and hammered out an e-mail.

Hey Sherlock,
The turkey tail is safe. What did Jillian say?
Call me!!!!!!!!!
Watson

Just as he hit SEND, he heard a bellow of pain. Brian ran
to the window and looked outside. His dad was hopping
around in the backyard holding his nose. Brian opened
the window.

"Are you okay?" he asked.

"Just a little miscommunication with the mud dauber,"
said Bruce Bain. "A natural hymenopteran defense mecha-
nism—nothing to worry about!"

"You got stung?"

"Yes, I got stung."

"I guess I just think the bluff should be left the way it is. At
least until Dr. Dart has a chance to finish his investigation."
Roni sipped her kiwi-strawberry-flavored iced tea. She had
decided against a grape slushy—they were better for dump-
ing on people than for drinking.

"I thought he already did that," Eric said.

They were sitting at the picnic table in front of the Quik
Mart. Eric had bought himself a cherry slushy.

"He wasn't finished. Also, I think condos are ugly."

"People have to live someplace," Eric said. "And it's not
like nobody ever built up on the bluffs before. There's that
development up on Wazoo Bluff."

"Wazoo Bluff wasn't a one-of-a-kind incredibly old and important burial ground like Indian Bluff."

Eric laughed.

"What's so funny?"

"You are. Indian Bluff is just another bluff. I don't know where you get this burial ground stuff."

"I get it from being in that cave and seeing the skeleton!"

"Yeah, well, the cave's gone. Besides, it was probably just some guy crawled in there and died. You don't even know for sure it was an Indian."

"I know it should be checked out before your dad starts digging into the bluff."

"I wouldn't worry about it," Eric said, looking away.

Roni slurped the bottom of her drink. "I *am* worried."

"Let's talk about something else."

"Like what?"

Eric looked blank, then said, "I don't know. You think of something."

"Read any good books lately?" she asked.

"I don't really read much. Not my thing."

"Oh, what do you like to do?" she asked, giving him another chance.

"Oh, you know, nothing much, the usual. Watch TV, hang out, listen to music, check out babes."

Roni decided to let "check out babes" slide. "Who do you like music-wise?"

"I don't really pay much attention. Whatever's on the radio. I listen to that one local station. It's pretty good."

She stared at him. He didn't even know the name of any of his favorite bands. He didn't read books.

"You want another drink?" he asked.

"No, thanks." Roni sat staring at Eric. Yes, he was cute. But he was also patronizing and annoying, and he had locked her in a secret passageway without being too concerned what happened to her. But worst of all, he was boring. Boring canceled out cute every time.

All the rest she could overlook, but boring was impossible.

"I've gotta get home and do some important laundry," she said.

27

aston larue

As soon as Roni got home, she checked her e-mail, found the message from Brian and called him.

"Watson?"

"Holmes!"

Roni thought of telling him about her slushy date with Eric, but she didn't think he'd understand. Plus they had more important things to talk about. "Has Jillian Greystone shown up to confiscate the turkey tail yet?"

"No . . . do you think she will?"

"She was pretty mad when you ran off like that. But I don't think she'll find you anytime soon. I told her your name was Aston LaRue."

"You told her my name was *Aston*?"

"It was the first thing that popped into my head. I couldn't believe it when you took off like that."

"I didn't know what else to do. Dr. Dart made me swear to protect the turkey tail. And he told me that Jillian Greystone will never forgive him. I guess we know why now."

"It was probably the plastic coffee mugs. Did he say anything else?"

"He was still pretty confused last time I saw him. But I learned something from his doctor. He said it looked like Dr. Dart had been hit on the head with a pipe or something."

118

"So he *was* attacked! I bet Fred Bloodwater was behind it."

"Or Jillian Greystone," Brian said. "She probably wants to claim the bones of Yorick for her own."

"If that's what she wants, then why would she blow up the cave? Now she can't get in there, either."

"Unless she had to seal the cave to cover up evidence that she attacked Dr. Dart. I wish we could get in there."

"Well, we can't." Roni felt as if they'd reached a dead end. And only two days till the bulldozers arrived.

Brian said, "Hey, what happened with Eric that made you give him a public slushing?"

"He locked me in a secret passage. Bloodwater House is riddled with them."

"No kidding? I love secret passages."

"You would. I think they might once have been for the servants. Or maybe the original Bloodwaters used them to spy on each other. If I hadn't run into Eric's little brothers, I might still be in there."

"He just left you?"

"That's why I slushed him. And when I tried to talk to him about Indian Bluff, he just laughed. He's such a jerk."

"You figured that out, huh?"

"I'm afraid he's right about one thing, though—we might not be able to stop the bulldozers. Fred Bloodwater has persuaded the city to invest a whole bunch of money with him. The mayor is totally in his pocket. Even my mom is pro-development."

"Maybe we should go to the newspaper. Show them the turkey tail and tell them where we got it."

"That wouldn't help. Without Dr. Dart, we can't prove the turkey tail came from the cave. Do you think there's any chance he'll get better in the next day or so?"

"I wouldn't count on it," Brian said. "Last time I saw him, he was calling me Dr. Brain. And eating rocks."

28

bat-poop breeze

"What is it?" Brian asked.

"Split pea soup," said his father.

"It looks kind of thick."

"Yes, the starches in the peas, when exposed to sufficient heat, act as a thickener." Bruce Bain gave the pot of green semi-liquid a stir.

"How come you decided to make pea soup?" Brian asked. He did not always appreciate his father's kitchen experiments, and this one was particularly *green*.

"It was the mud dauber," said his father, pointing at an angry red knob on the end of his nose. "As I was observing the way it gathered mud to build its nest, I began to think about the various ways water can homogenize with organic solids to form malleable, semi-liquid suspensions such as mud, concrete, glue and—"

Brian interrupted. "You were thinking about glue, so you decided to make soup?"

"Yes," said Bruce Bain.

Brian's mom came in through the back door, tipped her head back and sniffed.

"Mmm. What's for dinner?" she asked.

"It's one of dad's science experiments," Brian said.

"It smells delicious!" Mrs. Bain always praised her husband's cooking, no matter what.

"Look," said Mr. Bain, "I can insert the spoon into the soup and the viscosity holds it straight up and down. Remarkable!"

Mrs. Bain said, "Hmm. When will this viscous concoction be ready to eat?"

Mr. Bain tried to take out the spoon and nearly lifted the entire pot off the stove. Holding the pot down with one hand, he extracted the spoon with a tremendous sucking sound.

"I might need to thin it down a little," he said. "Give me ten minutes."

Smiling and shaking her head, Mrs. Bain began to set the table.

"Hey, Mom," Brian said. "You know that cave?"

"You didn't go in there again, did you?" she said as she set out three plates and three soup bowls.

"No! But it's not there anymore."

Mrs. Bain stopped what she was doing. "What do you mean?"

"Somebody blew it up."

Mrs. Bain put on her stern, efficient detective face and waited for more.

"Roni and I went up to Indian Bluff this morning to . . . to look for Indian artifacts."

Mrs. Bain raised one eyebrow and crossed her arms.

"And while we were there, we heard this explosion. We

went to check it out, and the cave was gone. The entrance is completely collapsed."

"I see."

"It was, like, dynamited or something."

"Dynamited?" She frowned. "How do you know it didn't just cave in?"

"It was really loud."

"Hmm. Maybe the contractor was getting a head start on the development. I'll have to call Bob Necropoli, our forensics expert. He was planning to drive down from St. Paul to take a look at that skeleton you saw. I suppose we'll have to wait until next week and get an excavation crew. We can find out then whether the cave-in was natural or not."

"Next week is too late! They're going to bulldoze the bluff on Friday!"

"I don't see how the one thing affects the other."

"They'll be ripping into the bluff. They could cause the entire cave to collapse!"

Mrs. Bain took a moment to digest that, then shook her head wearily. "We'll just have to take a chance on that. Mayor Berglund will pop a blood vessel if we halt construction on his pet project. As for the skeleton, from what you've told me it was quite old. I don't see what difference a few days will make."

"But Mom, Dr. Dart thinks the whole bluff is really important! It could be a burial ground or something."

Mrs. Bain was shaking her head in a way that Brian knew meant he had hit a brick wall.

"Just a second," he said, and he ran up to his room. He was back half a minute later with the turkey tail. "Dr. Dart gave me this. He found it in the cave. It's really old and valuable."

Mrs. Bain took the stone and examined it, then gave Brian a look he did not like at all. "We got a call a little while ago from the college," she said. "They called to report the theft of a valuable artifact from the college's collection."

Brian had a bad, bad feeling.

Mrs. Bain said, "The woman who called said the missing item was a type of projectile point called a turkey tail, and that it was last seen in the possession of a boy named Aston LaRue." She placed the stone carefully beside her soup bowl. "I don't suppose you know Mr. LaRue?"

Roni, sitting at her computer, frowned at the list on her screen.

Lie down in front of the bulldozers
Chain self to tree on bluff
Threaten to jump off bluff if they start bulldozing
Pull up all surveyor's stakes so they don't know where to dig
Kidnap Eric Bloodwater

Was there anything there that would work? None of the tactics she imagined would do more than delay the development for a few hours. Kidnapping Eric might slow them down for a few days, but eventually she would get caught and thrown in jail and they'd build the condos anyway. Violence, vandalism and self-sacrifice would not solve the problem—but what else was available to her?

She typed another list.

Information
Imagination
Intelligence
Persuasiveness

Those were her tools. With the right Information she could use her Imagination, Intelligence and Persuasiveness to persuade them to stop—or at least delay—the ground breaking on Friday. But who was "them"? Who had the power to stop the bulldozers?

She opened a new document and began a third list.

Fred Bloodwater
Buddy Berglund
Bloodwater College
The Bloodwater Police

Roni stared at each of her lists, clicking from window to window, waiting for inspiration. She kept going back to the middle list, her list of tools. She couldn't make herself any more Intelligent or Persuasive—not by Friday—but she could use her Imagination to get more Information.

It sucks being a kid, Brian thought. He laced his fingers be-hind his head and stared up at the hundreds of Pokémon cards glued to the ceiling of his bedroom.

If he were an adult, they would have to listen to him. Not that his mom didn't listen—but she didn't *listen*. Sure, she believed him when he told her that Dr. Dart had given him the turkey tail. And she had believed him about the skeleton in the cave. And she half believed him when he told her somebody had caved-in the cave on purpose.

What she *didn't* believe was how important it was. She thought the bulldozers were no big deal, and that he was getting hysterical over nothing. She heard what he was *say-ing,* but she just didn't *get* it.

Because he was a kid. And because she hadn't taken a sol-emn oath with her hand on the skull of a long-dead Indian. His hand still remembered the smooth, moisture-sucking dryness of that old yellow skull.

He scowled at the cards stuck to his ceiling. When he'd been about eight years old, he'd had the idea to glue all his Pokémon cards up there. He had borrowed his dad's glue gun, hauled a stepladder up to his room and started gluing. When his mom had seen what he had done, she had said, "You're the one who's going to have to look at them every night for the next ten years, kiddo."

Stupid Pokémon cards.

He closed his eyes and thought about all the skulls he had seen. The petrified skull of a dinosaur. The skull and crossbones on a pirate's flag. The skull of a tiger with its three-inch teeth. What would be really cool, he thought—better than Pokémon—would be skull cards. Cards with the skulls of famous people and interesting animals. Like anteaters. What would the skull of an anteater look like? Or a bat. Bats probably have really cool skulls.

Bats.

What about the bats?

A sick feeling hit him right in the stomach. He imagined the thousands of bats trapped in the cave slowly starving to death. How long could a bat go without food? He imagined them dropping from the ceiling, one by one. Plop. Plop.

Plop.

Maybe the bats weren't trapped. They would need only the tiniest crack. Maybe they could squeeze out past the rubble.

He remembered standing up there staring at the pile of rock where the cave entrance had collapsed. It had looked as if the entire passage had collapsed in on itself. He didn't think there were any cracks at all.

Then he thought about the first time he had stood on that ledge looking into the cave. He had felt a cool breeze coming from the cave's mouth. A bat-poop-scented breeze.

Brian sat up in bed.

The bat-poop breeze! If air came rushing out of the cave, it had to be getting in somehow.

Somewhere on Indian Bluff was a second entrance to the cave.

29

information

Roni opened her favorite search engine and typed in "Eric Bloodwater."

Nothing.

She tried "Poophead." Nine thousand forty-six hits.

"Fred Bloodwater" produced only a few articles from the *Bloodwater Clarion*—the same old news items about the development.

That was odd.

Eric had told her that his dad had done all sorts of developments. If that were true, she should have gotten more hits. Developers usually made the local news.

She tried entering his name as "Frederick Bloodwater." No hits.

F. Bloodwater. Nope.

She tried Frederico, Fredwick and Freddie. Zippo, nada, zilch.

She sat back in her chair and thought hard. Had Eric been lying about his dad's real estate experience? It seemed unlikely that Fred Bloodwater's name hadn't popped up *anywhere*. She wondered if the city council had checked out his background before investing all that money with him.

She found her mother watching *Antiques Roadshow* and

eating popcorn in the den. Roni helped herself to a handful of popcorn.

"They just valued a pre–Civil War slave quilt at a hundred thousand dollars," Nick said. "Maybe we have something like that in the basement."

"Are we descended from slaves?"

"I don't think so. Oh! Would you look at that vase!" She grabbed Roni's arm. "It's so ugly, it *has* to be Lalique."

Roni extracted her arm from her mother's grasp. Nick could get a little weird during *Antiques Roadshow.*

"Nick, I just did an Internet search for Fred Bloodwater and—"

"Those Lalique vases can be worth tens of thousands of dollars."

"I am on the edge of my seat," Roni said in a flat robot voice.

Nick laughed. "Gimme a break, kiddo. I have to listen to that stuff you call music." She looked at her daughter. "Did you need something?"

"Yes. I was wondering if anybody checked into Fred Bloodwater. I mean, I couldn't find anything about him on the Net. Did anybody do a background check on him?"

"There was no need, dear. The man had a *suitcase* full of news clippings about himself and his company, as well as several letters of recommendation. One of the letters was from the governor of California! Besides, he's a *Bloodwater.* Why do you ask?"

"Because—"

Nick gasped and grabbed Roni's arm again. "It's a counterfeit! The poor woman thought she had a fifty-thousand-dollar vase and it turns out to be a fake!"

"You're hurting my arm, Nick."

"Oh!" Nick released her. "Sorry. I just get upset when I see that. There are so many frauds and liars in this world. I'm sorry, dear, what were you asking me?"

"Never mind," Roni said as a new thought struck her. "I'll get back to you."

Brian reached the bluff road just as the sun disappeared below the horizon. Several large yellow machines were lined up along the dirt road—two bulldozers, a backhoe, a road grader and two dump trucks. Tomorrow morning they would be tearing up the bluff. All that weight and vibration might cause the caverns in the bluff to collapse. Tonight was his last chance to put a stop to the development.

He walked his bike to the edge of the precipice, sat down and looked out over the shadowed river valley. If they built those condos, whoever bought them would have a spectacular view.

"Fancy meeting you here!" It was Jillian Greystone.

Startled, Brian jumped straight up.

She stepped toward him, and her hand clamped hard on his arm.

30

bat patrol

"Careful! It's a long ways down," said Jillian.

"What . . . what are you doing here?" Brian asked.

"Trespassing, same as you." She released his arm. "Actually, I thought I'd take one last look around, since Andrew isn't able to do it for himself." She kicked one of the orange-flagged surveyor's stakes. "After tomorrow this will all be torn up."

"Did you find anything?"

Jillian shook her head. "Not even a piece of pottery. And certainly not a turkey tail." She gave him a hard look. "It seems you have the only one in Bloodwater."

"Not anymore. My mom took it."

"I hope she is planning to return it to the college."

Brian nodded.

Jillian smiled. "Good. I really don't know what Andrew was thinking. I'm lucky I found out how obsessive he was before I went ahead and married him." She kicked at the dirt. "Indian Bluff—what a joke! You know, nearly all the bluffs in the area have—or rather, *had*—burial mounds or other signs of Native American presence, but not this one." She laughed. "Ironic, isn't it? That they named it Indian Bluff?"

"I guess so."

"And what about you, Aston LaRue? What are you doing up here? Looking for another turkey tail?"

For a few seconds, Brian considered telling her about his theory, but he decided he couldn't trust her.

"Just hanging," Brian said, giving her his best all-purpose answer. Jillian seemed to accept it.

"I'm heading back," she said. "It's getting too dark to see much. Do you need a lift?"

"No, thanks."

As soon as Jillian was out of sight, Brian felt the confidence drain out of him. Suddenly his great idea did not seem so great. The other entrance to the cave could be fifty feet away, or half a mile. And even if he found it, the opening might be too small for him to squeeze through.

But not too small for a bat.

Brian slowly turned in a circle, scanning the sky. It was still light out, but growing darker by the minute.

A flicker of movement caught his eye—but it was only a bird.

He kept searching, rotating like a radar dish. Again he saw something in the air, but it disappeared into the coulee. There. A black shape fluttered by like a scrap of crepe paper in a whirlwind, in and out of sight in a heartbeat. Definitely a bat. But where had it come from?

A few seconds later, he saw another one. It had seemed to come from down in the coulee. Brian turned his attention in that direction.

There was still light in the sky, but in the shadows of the

coulee it was as dark as night. Brian switched on his flashlight and lowered himself down a tumbled slope of mossy boulders. Every few seconds he stopped and shone his light around, hoping to see a bat emerge from some crack or crevice.

In the end, it was his ears, not his eyes, that led him on. A faint chittering and squeaking drew him into a treacherous tangle of fallen trees and slippery boulders. He recognized the enormous boulder he'd been standing on when the cave had been dynamited. He circled the boulder, moved farther down the coulee, then stopped and listened again.

Now the high-pitched sounds seemed to be coming from above him. He started back up, going around the boulder on the opposite side, but was blocked by a second boulder almost as large as the first. Could he fit between them? He sent the beam of his flashlight into the space between the boulders and was startled by two bats coming straight at his face.

He let out a yelp and ducked. He could hear the whisper of the bats' wings as they skimmed over his head.

Making his way around the smaller boulder, Brian climbed onto it from the uphill side, lay on his belly and shined his light straight down into the opening. It was a zig-zag crack about four feet long by a little more than a foot wide—big enough to squeeze into—but from what he could see, the shaft dropped straight down, like a well. Easy to get into, but not so easy to climb back out of.

He watched several more bats emerge in ones and twos, then took out his dad's cell phone and punched in Roni's number.

31

back door

Roni began by Googling Eric's secret name, "Fenton Blood-water."

Zero hits. She tried entering just "Fenton" and got 2,600,000 hits, too many to sort through.

What had SamOwen said their parents' secret names were? Fitzroy and Camillia? How many Fitzroys could there be? She typed in "Fitzroy" and got 700,000 hits. Too many. She tried "Fitzroy Bloodwater." Zippo. Likewise for "Camillia Bloodwater."

Roni sat back and scowled at her computer. For a few minutes there she had hoped that the Bloodwater twins' silly secret names might be more than a game. But Fitzroy and Camillia Bloodwater were just as absent from cyberspace as Fred Bloodwater was.

Frustrated, Roni began Googling everything she could think of—"Bloodwater Development," "Ridgewood Residences," "Bloodwater+Fitzroy" and "Fitzroy+Development." She either got nothing, or too much, or just a bunch of articles from the *Clarion* that she had already seen.

Then she did a search for "Fitzroy+Camillia."

Thirty hits. The first one was a baby-name site. The second site was devoted to British genealogy. The third listing took her to a nine-month-old article in the archives of a

California newspaper called the *Redwood Valley Sun-Times*. She opened the article: "Valley Couple Sought in Riverwood Estates Case." She stared at the accompanying photograph for a full thirty seconds before reading the article. When she had finished reading, she looked at the photo again, and a grim smile spread slowly across her face.

VALLEY COUPLE SOUGHT IN LAND FRAUD

Police raided the home of a Redwood Valley couple Thursday night searching for evidence in the Riverwood Estates land fraud case. The couple, identified by police as Fitzroy and Camillia Oraczko, were not at home. They are believed to have left the Redwood Valley area.

"The Oraczkos have robbed us, pure and simple," said Mayor Winston Barnes. "The Riverwood Estates development has cost our city millions."

Using the names Jordan and Vivian Sutter, the Oraczkos and their three children arrived in Redwood Valley last September, claiming to be descendants of John Sutter, the owner of Sutter's Mill, where gold was first discovered in California. The Oraczkos persuaded the Redwood Valley City Council to support their plans for an extensive housing development in the west valley.

Construction was begun two weeks ago when sections of the west valley, including thirty acres of young redwoods, were leveled by bulldozers. Work

> was halted when it was discovered that the "Sutters" had disappeared, along with the $2.3 million they had borrowed from the city.

The photo with the article was a very nice shot of a smiling man and a woman standing in front of a bulldozer.

They looked exactly like Mr. and Mrs. Bloodwater.

The thing about cell phones was that sometimes when you really needed to make a call, you couldn't. Brian had to climb back up out of the coulee to the top of the bluff to get a signal. He punched in Roni's number again. She picked up on the first ring.

"The game's afoot," said Brian.

"Watson? Is that you?"

"Yes. The game's afoot."

"The what's a what?"

"That's a quote from Sherlock Holmes," Brian said.

"Oh. Hey, you won't believe what I just found!"

"You won't believe what *I* just found."

"Mine's better."

"Not a chance, Sherlock. Listen, I need you to hop on Hillary and come out here to the bluff right now."

"Now? It's, like, almost ten o'clock."

"Bring rope—lots of it—a flashlight, a big ball of string, a camera and—"

"Wait—you got into the cave?"

"I found the back door."

32

spelunking

The ball of string and the flashlight were easy, and she could buy a disposable camera at the Quik Mart, but where would she find rope? She didn't want to ask Nick, who was still in the den watching PBS. Asking Nick would lead to too many questions.

Maybe in the basement. Just as she was heading down the stairs, the phone rang. Roni ran back up the steps and picked up the kitchen extension.

"Roni?" It was Eric Bloodwater. Or whatever his name was, really.

"Hi," she said.

"What are you doing?"

"Looking for rope."

"Oh. I just wanted to say, I'm really sorry about the secret passage thing. And it was fun hanging with you today."

"Uh, yeah, me, too. Listen, I have to be someplace. I can't talk much."

"Are you going to a rodeo or a hanging?"

"Huh?"

"You know. You said you were looking for rope."

"I'm going spelunking." Roni figured there was no way Eric—or rather, Fenton—would know that spelunking meant "to explore a cave." She was right.

He said, "If you don't want to tell me . . ."

Roni instantly regretted having said anything at all. "Look, I gotta go. Let's talk tomorrow, okay?"

After hanging up, Roni made a quick search of the basement. No rope. She tried the garage and found a small piece of rope hanging from the wall, but not nearly enough. Closing the garage door, she noticed that the lights were on in Mr. Billig's garage, and the door was open.

Perfect. Mr. Billig was the handiest guy in the neighborhood. He had tools like dogs have hair. If anybody had rope, it would be him.

Mr. Billig's legs were sticking out from under his cherry-red 1965 Corvette. A radio balanced on the hood was blasting moldy oldies. Mr. Billig sang along as he worked on his car.

"Mr. Billig?" Roni said.

". . . fun fun fun . . . ," Mr. Billig sang.

Roni raised her voice. "Hello?"

". . . till her daddy took her T-Bird awayeyay!"

Roni turned off the radio.

"Hey!" Mr. Billig shouted. He wriggled out from beneath his car. "Oh, it's you, Roni."

"Hi, Mr. Billig."

"Hi yourself." Mr. Billig climbed creakily to his feet. He was a small, thin man with a wrinkled, suntanned face and ears that stood straight out. According to Nick, Mr. Billig had gotten stuck being who he was back in the 1960s and just couldn't get out. He seemed happy enough.

"I was wondering if I could borrow some rope."

"Rope? What kind of rope?"

"Like the kind of rope you could climb."

Mr. Billig scratched his head. "Rope. Rope. Lesseee . . ." He closed his eyes and scrunched up his already scrunchy face and thought for a moment. Then his eyes popped open and he looked straight up. "Aha!"

Roni tipped her head back and saw, hanging from the rafters, a coil of thick rope.

"Tow rope," Mr. Billig said. "About a hundred feet. That do ya?"

"I hope so," Roni said.

Ten minutes later, with the heavy coil of rope looped over her shoulder, Roni pulled up to the Quik Mart. She parked her Vespa and walked into the store, still wearing the coil of rope.

"Gonna tie something up, or is that the latest teen fashion?" asked the old man behind the counter.

"Neither," Roni said. "Do you have any disposable cameras? With a flash?"

"I got all kinds," said the man. He pointed at the wall behind the counter, where several types of cameras were displayed. "Take your pick."

Roni heard the door buzzer go off.

"Do any of them have an extra-strong flash?" she asked. "I'll be taking pictures inside a really dark place."

"Don't know." The clerk set one of each variety on the counter. Roni sensed someone standing behind her, waiting.

"I'll take this one." Roni handed the clerk a twenty.

Thump, thump, thump. What was that noise? Was the person behind her bouncing a ball or something?

The clerk rang up her purchase. "So what's the rope for?" he asked.

"I'm going caving," Roni said.

"At night?" said the clerk.

"What's the difference?" Roni said. "Either way, it's dark in there."

Thump, thump.

Roni grabbed her change and the camera. She turned and almost ran smack into Professor Bloom.

"Good evening, Miss Delicata," he said, thumping the rubber tip of his cane on the floor.

"Hi, Professor," Roni said.

Professor Bloom stared at her for the longest five seconds Roni had ever endured.

"We will be touring the county courthouse tomorrow," he finally said, setting a carton of milk and a box of bran flakes on the counter. "I will see you there, I trust."

Roni made her escape and a minute later was back on Hillary, heading up Highway 61 toward Indian Bluff.

33

banshee

Brian squatted near the hole, shining his flashlight at the opening. He didn't want to get too close. Bats were still coming out every now and then. He hoped they would stop before Roni arrived.

He was counting the amount of time between bats. It had been nearly five minutes since he had seen one. Maybe they had all gone out for the evening.

He leaned over the hole and shone his flashlight down into it. Not much to see. He thought he could make out the bottom, but he wasn't sure. As he moved the flashlight, he could see shadows arranging themselves. There was an earth floor about thirty feet below him.

Suddenly he felt hands on his shoulders. He let out a yell and almost fell forward into the hole. The hands pulled him back just in time. He heard Roni's laugh.

Brian twisted free and stood up. "Not funny!" he said. First Jillian, and now Roni had scared him the same way. It was getting old. Although, if it had been him sneaking up on Roni, it would have been hilarious.

"Funny." Roni turned her flashlight on and shined it into his face. "I totally got you. You screamed like a banshee."

"What is a banshee, anyway?"

"I have no idea." Roni aimed the beam of her flashlight into the hole. "Are you really going down there?"

"Me? I thought we were both going!"

"Shouldn't somebody wait up here? Just in case?"

"Just in case what?"

"You know—bears, cave trolls, vampire bats, troglo-dytes . . ."

"Okay, okay. I'll go down first and check things out. If there are no cave trolls or troglodytes, you can come down, too."

"We'll see," said Roni.

Brian took the rope from her and dropped it down until he could see the end touch the cave floor. He wrapped the other end twice around a nearby tree and tied it with a sailor's knot.

"Very impressive," said Roni. "I didn't know you were a Boy Scout."

"My dad taught me that one," Brian said. He pocketed his flashlight, grabbed the rope and sat down with his feet hang-ing into the cave entrance. "Want to give me some light?"

Roni shined her flashlight past him. "Give my regards to the cave troll."

Brian hated that exercise in gym class when they had to try to climb up a thick rope about nine thousand feet to the ceil-ing. He tried to miss that day of school if he knew it was coming up. One time he had managed to get about twenty feet up before his fingers gave out. He had slid back down and burned his hands.

But lowering himself into the cave turned out to be relatively easy. The rocky, uneven walls of the shaft gave him plenty of places to brace himself. He stopped and rested halfway down.

"You okay?" Roni asked.

"Piece of cake," Brian said. "You could almost do this without a rope."

"See any scary man-eating creatures yet?"

"Just a few. Nothing I can't handle." Brian continued to climb down, gripping the rope with his hands and bracing his feet against the walls.

A few feet farther down, the shaft suddenly widened, and he found himself swinging free, supporting his entire weight with his hands on the rope. He lowered himself quickly, his hands slipping painfully on the rope, until his feet hit the floor.

Roni's voice echoed down through the shaft. "Brian?"

"I'm good," he yelled, turning on his flashlight.

He was in a dome-shaped chamber about thirty feet across, its ceiling studded with fat, limey stalagtites. Large flat chunks of limestone littered the floor. The opening of the shaft was a good ten feet above him. It would be tough to climb back up the rope, but he thought he could do it.

Not that he had any choice.

But could Roni climb a rope like that? He wasn't so sure.

"You better stay up there!" he yelled.

"Okay!" She sounded relieved.

Brian ran the beam of his flashlight around the chamber and found two openings, both large enough for him to fit through.

The shaft he had entered was directly north of the cave entrance that had been dynamited. He took out his compass and took a reading. One of the two openings was roughly to the south. Brian shined his light into it just as a bat came flying out. Brian ducked. The bat careened through the chamber and shot up the shaft. Brian heard a startled yelp come from Roni. He laughed, then followed the beam of his flashlight into the passageway.

"Brian?" Roni shouted. Her voice was swallowed by the shaft.

No answer. Roni wasn't too surprised. He'd been gone only six minutes. She wondered how long she should wait before calling 911. An hour? Two?

She slapped at something biting the back of her neck. An hour in the woods was a long time. She sat down a few feet from the opening with her back against a tree trunk.

Time.

Passed.

Slowly.

She played the beam of her flashlight across the trees and boulders. The shadows just made the woods look darker and scarier, so she turned it off.

She checked her watch. Three more minutes had passed. She shined the flashlight on her feet. Maybe she should figure out a better way to tie shoes. Why did the knot always have to go at the top? Why not put the knot down at the toe?

She heard a crunching noise and turned off the flashlight, her heart pounding.

The noise was coming from higher in the coulee.

Probably just a deer.

Or a bear.

She saw a flicker of light coming through the trees. That made it a human—but who? Somebody just decided to take a walk in the woods? In the middle of the night? On Indian Bluff?

It could be whoever attacked Dr. Dart, Roni thought. It could be whoever blew up the cave.

Whoever it was, they were coming straight toward her.

She looked around for a place to hide. If she moved far, they would hear her. Maybe she could hide in the cave entrance—just go down a few feet.

The person with the flashlight was only about fifty feet away. It looked like they might walk right past her, if she could get out of sight.

This is no time to think, Roni told herself. It's time to act.

She put her flashlight in her pocket, grabbed the rope and carefully lowered herself into the jagged opening. Brian was right—it was easier than it looked. She climbed down about six feet, then braced her back against the rock and found toeholds for her feet in the opposite wall. She could sit there for quite a while before getting tired.

But then she started thinking about two things: one, the person with the flashlight could see her if he looked down the hole, and two, what about the bats? She did not like the idea of bats trying to squeeze past her in the narrow shaft. In fact, the more she thought about it, the more she wanted to scream.

There was only one thing to do: continue on down the shaft.

Slowly, she let herself down the rope, supporting most of the weight by feeling for toeholds on the walls. This is so easy, she thought.

And then her feet were suddenly pedaling air. Frantically, she sought a toehold, but the shaft had widened and she was hanging by her hands. She tried to wrap her legs around the rope, but she couldn't find it in the dark.

Her hands were slipping. Roni squeezed the rope as hard as she could, ignoring the pain in her hands. She knew she couldn't hold on for long, and then suddenly it didn't matter anymore—

—because she was falling.

34

brain surgery

It would be easy to get lost, Brian thought as he entered yet another chamber that looked just like the one he'd been in five minutes before. The cave was like a bunch of big bubbles in the earth connected by numerous twisted, narrow, bewildering passageways.

In fact, he wasn't 100 percent sure how to get back to the entrance. But that didn't mean he was *lost*. He wasn't actually *lost* until he tried to find his way back and couldn't.

Brian played the flashlight beam over the walls and across the dusty floor.

Footprints!

He examined them carefully. They looked familiar. Brian lifted his right foot and looked at the tread pattern.

Yep. Same shoe. Either there had been someone else in the cave wearing identical sneakers, or he was going in circles.

Even with his compass he was confused. Was it possible that this cave didn't hook up with the other cave? Maybe there were two completely separate caverns.

Brian didn't believe it. The two cave entrances were only about a hundred yards apart. They had to be connected. He ran his flashlight beam slowly around the chamber. No other way out. He shook his head and went back the way he had come.

For about three long seconds, Roni lay in the dark thinking that she had broken every bone in her body. She thought her heart had stopped. A bunch of white lights were floating in front of her face. The lights began to whirl and she felt as if she were being sucked into a whirlpool, and for a moment she was certain she was about to die.

Then she remembered to breathe.

As air filled her lungs, the lights disappeared and her head stopped spinning. She sat up in the utter darkness and listened to the echoey silence.

She looked up. She had to be sitting directly beneath the shaft. There. The faintest imaginable light. A single star.

What had happened? She had been hanging on to the rope and suddenly her hands had just given up. Remembering the flashlight in her pocket, Roni took it out and switched it on.

She was in a chamber about the size of a classroom. She looked around quickly, checking for cave bears and trolls.

She seemed to be alone. Just her, and the dangling rope, and a bunch of rocks scattered on the floor. She was lucky she hadn't landed on one. She shined the light to where the rope disappeared into the shaft, five feet above her head. Could she climb back up into the shaft? Maybe if she held on to the rope and climbed up on Brian's shoulders she could pull herself up.

Maybe.

But first she had to find Brian. She looked around the

chamber again and found an opening leading into a passageway. She shined her light into the passage. Dark. That was the problem with caves. Too much dark.

Brian came across his own stupid footprints four times before he finally noticed an opening he hadn't seen before. At first he thought the six-inch-wide crack was too small to fit through. He shined his light into the crack and saw that it got wider.

Might as well try, he thought. Turning sideways, he tried to wedge himself into the crack, but his chest was too wide. He took a couple of deep breaths, then blew all the air out of his lungs and tried again.

It worked! He was squeezing through, almost as if the wall was swallowing him, when his shirt caught on a projecting chunk of rock. Brian panicked. He was stuck in a crevice with no air in his lungs. He closed his eyes and tried to will himself smaller, then pushed hard with his legs. He heard his shirt rip, the pressure on his chest eased and he sucked air into his lungs.

He had made it. The bad news was that he'd have to do it again to get back out. Oh well, he would deal with that when the time came.

The new passageway quickly widened. For the first time, Brian found footprints that were not his own. Yes! He followed the footprints.

The passageway led to another chamber. Had he been here before? Brian shined his flashlight around. At first pass, he didn't see anything. Then when he played the flashlight around the chamber more slowly, he saw something in the far corner. He jumped into the chamber and ran over to the scattered collection of bones.

Dr. Dart's rescuers had been none too kind to poor Yorick. His bones had been scattered and trampled as the rescue workers had put the injured archaeologist on a stretcher and carried him out of the cave. A few yards from the scattered bones he found the skull hiding behind a tumble of rocks. Brian picked up the skull, saying, "Don't bite me or anything, Yorick. It's me, the guy who swore an oath on your stupid bony head."

Yorick grinned up at him. Brian was glad the skull had a name—it made it not quite so grisly. He set the skull against the wall by the bones, then took out the disposable flash camera Roni had given him. Holding the flashlight and the camera at the same time, he framed the shot of the bones with the skull in the exact center, then hit the button.

The flash lit up the cavern.

But what was that? Brian thought he had seen an odd glare in Yorick's skull. He took a step to the side and photographed the scene from a different angle.

Again, the odd glare. He bent over the skull and shined his light into Yorick's empty eye sockets. He could see through to the back of the skull. But what was that shiny thing?

He picked up the skull and turned it around. On the back of the skull, part of the bone had been replaced by a shiny steel plate the size of a half-dollar.

Brian stared at the metal patch for several seconds. Did

ancient Native Americans do brain surgery? Possibly. But did they have steel? Brian thought about the turkey tail on his desk at home and shook his head. Anybody who had to make arrowheads out of rocks would not be able to patch a skull with stainless steel.

There was only one possible conclusion. Whoever Yorick had been, he wasn't ancient. He probably wasn't even an Indian.

Stupid Yorick. Probably just some old prospector who had wandered into the cave and died. Brian looked more closely at the pile of bones and saw something else—a black rubber cup about the size of a shot glass. Brian picked it up, trying to think what it was. It looked familiar.

Whatever it was, it was definitely not Native American.

So much for their saving an "Indian burial ground" from the bulldozers.

He shrugged and added the rubber cup to the collection in his pocket, then started back toward the cave entrance—if he could find it.

I do not like caves, Roni thought to herself as she inched her way along the passage. I do not like caves and I do not like secret passages. I do not like them at all. And if I see one more bat, I am going to scream my lungs out.

The passage opened into another chamber much like the first. Only now there were two more openings. One might lead to Brian, the other to a bottomless pit, or worse.

"Brian?" she called out. "Hello?" Her voice echoed briefly,

then died. She examined the floor and found footprints going in and out of both exits. Great. Maybe she should go back to the entrance and wait for him to show up.

Roni was still standing there, undecided, when she heard a faint noise on her left. She switched off her flashlight, pressed her back to the wall and waited.

A few seconds later she saw a flashlight beam shine from the passageway, followed by Brian, wriggling out from a narrow crack in the wall. He was only a few feet away from her.

What sound would a bear make? As soon as he was free of the opening, she let out a roar that sounded more like a sick cat than a cave bear, but worked perfectly. Brian yelped and jumped like a Pogo stick.

Roni almost fell down laughing.

"That's not funny!" Brian said.

"Yes it is," Roni said, still laughing.

"Okay, okay," Brian said after a second. "Maybe it's a *little* funny." He shined his light around the chamber. "Say, do you know the way back?"

"As a matter of fact, I do. Did you find Yorick?"

"Yeah . . . only you're not going to like this."

"Like what?" Roni asked.

"Like, he has a metal plate in his skull."

She's taking this remarkably well, Brian thought as they moved slowly through the cramped passage, crouching to keep their heads from hitting the low ceiling.

Roni, a few feet ahead of him, said, "I wonder who he was."

"Who knows?" Brian said. "But whoever he was, I'll bet they won't stop the development to find out."

"Hey, I forgot to tell you! I figured out how to stop the bulldozers."

"You did?"

"Yeah. I found out that the Bloodwaters aren't really Bloodwaters. Their real name is Oraczko."

"Gesundheit," said Brian.

"No, I mean that's their name. Fitzroy and Camillia Oraczko."

"Fitzroy?" said Brian. "You're kidding."

"Seriously. I found it on the Web. He's been involved in a bunch of other real estate scams. It's all a plot to steal money from the city. I can prove it."

Brian thought for a moment. "If you already figured all that out, what the heck are we doing in this cave?"

"I thought you liked caves. Besides, we had to check out Yorick, right? And look for evidence of who attacked Dr. Dart. Did you find anything?"

"I don't know. Maybe. I—hey, are we here?"

They had reached the end of the passageway and entered a familiar-looking chamber.

"Ta-da!" Roni said. "Told you I knew how to get back."

Brian shined his flashlight around. This had to be the right chamber—but something was missing.

"Where's the rope?" he asked.

35

the black nose

"Rope?"

Roni looked up at the opening five feet above her head and her heart went *thunk*.

"Yeah," Brian said. "The rope. The thing we climbed down on. The thing we need so we can climb back out."

Roni looked up at the bottom of the shaft and shuddered. It was only five feet above her head, but with no rope it might as well be five miles.

"It was there when I left," she said.

For several seconds they stood in silence, both flashlight beams on the ropeless opening above them.

"Somebody must have pulled it up," Brian said.

"Good one, Watson. Do you have any other brilliant observations?"

"I wonder who."

"I did see somebody out there with a flashlight. That's why I climbed down here—so whoever it was wouldn't see me."

"Who do you think it was? Who knew we were here?"

Roni thought for a moment. "Eric, maybe," she said.

"You told Eric Bloodwater we were coming here? Are you nuts?"

"It wasn't like that. He called and . . ." Roni's voice got

small. ". . . I told him I was going spelunking. But I figured he wouldn't know what I was talking about." She added, "I suppose he could have looked it up."

"He's probably laughing himself to death right now," Brian said.

"We don't know for sure it was him. I also ran into Professor Bloom at the Quik Mart. He might have overheard me say something about caves when I was buying the camera."

"Why would Professor Bloom want to trap us in a cave?"

"Good point. So it was probably Eric, trapping me in another dark passageway. I'm going to kill him."

"Uh-oh," Brian said.

" 'Uh-oh' what?"

"Jillian Greystone. I saw her up on the bluff when I was waiting for the bats to come out. She might have hidden in the woods and spied on us. So at least three people knew we were here."

"Three that we know of. Not that it does us any good."

"Actually, it does help. One of them might eventually tell the police." Brian paused. "After we've been missing for a day or so."

"I'm hungry right now," Roni said.

Brian pulled something out of his pocket. "Care for a Tootsie Roll?"

Roni took the Tootsie Roll and put it in her pocket. "I'll save it for later." She shined her light on the opening above them. "Maybe if you climb up on my shoulders?"

"Not high enough," Brian said. "I don't suppose you have a ladder in your pocket?"

"I left my ladder at home. Hey, don't you have a phone?"

"Of course!" Brian pulled out his dad's cell phone and turned it on. He frowned.

"Let me guess," Roni said. "No signal."

Brian sat down on a chunk of limestone and switched off his flashlight. "Better turn yours off, too."

"Why?" Roni did not like the thought of sitting in the dark.

"Because we have to save our batteries. No telling how long we'll be in here."

Brian did his best thinking in the dark. He loved the way if he stared really hard in absolute darkness little floaters would appear. Especially if he closed his eyes and pressed on his eyeballs. He had read that the imaginary lights were called phosphenes. He liked to think of phosphenes as tiny idea berries ready to be plucked. One of them might know how to get out of this cave.

"Stop humming!" Roni said.

Brian started as if from a deep sleep. "Was I humming?"

"Yes, you were, and it's driving me crazy. Have you figured out how to make the ceiling lower?"

"No ... but hey! How about if we make the floor higher."

Roni didn't say anything for a few seconds. Then

she switched on her flashlight. "Good idea. We'd better get started."

They started by dragging all the loose rocks to the center of the chamber. The limestone chunks were mostly flat, like thick chunks of petrified peanut brittle. They shoved them all together to make an uneven platform directly beneath the hole.

"Well, that gets us about six inches closer," Brian said.

Roni looked around the chamber. "We're already out of rocks."

"Then let's get some more," Brian said as he ducked into the passageway.

Roni had never worked so hard in her entire life. Every rock had to be lifted and carried, rolled or dragged back through the passageway and added to the platform. The first few trips weren't so bad, but Roni's arms and back and legs soon began to burn and throb. But as the stone platform grew, Roni felt a fierce pride burning inside her.

This was no ordinary pile of rocks. This pile of rocks was going to save their lives.

Several times during the construction Brian tried to tell her it was high enough, but Roni kept saying no, it wasn't quite there. "I want you up on my shoulders only once."

Shortly after midnight, Roni found a squarish chunk of limestone about three inches thick and as big around as a manhole cover—the perfect cap for their lifesaving pile.

When she rolled it in, Brian was sitting cross-legged on

the pile of rocks, holding his flashlight in his lap. The beam shined straight up, giving his face a spooky, horror show look. For some reason his nose was black, totally black.

Roni pointed down at the slab. "Help me lift it up."

With much grunting and straining they managed to get the flat stone onto the top of the pile. They stepped back to admire their work, a pile almost as high as Brian was tall.

"It's beautiful," Roni said. "Okay, I'll bite. What is that *thing* on your nose?"

"I don't know." Brian removed the black object and handed it to her. "I found it back by Yorick's skeleton."

Roni looked at the small rubber cup. "It looks like one of those things you put on the leg of a chair to keep it from scratching the floor." Deep inside her brain, pieces clicked into place, gears meshed, doors opened.

"I know what this is!" she said.

At that exact moment, her flashlight went out.

"Uh-oh. I guess we'd better get out of here while we've still got one working flashlight," Brian said. His own flashlight was fading.

She climbed carefully onto the pile and stood on the flat stone at the top. A few of the rocks shifted slightly, then settled into place. Roni tipped her head back. The opening was so close she could reach up and touch it.

"Give me your light." She shined the beam up into the shaft. The light was too weak for her to see much of anything—then it died completely.

36

up and out

Brian didn't think he would ever try out for the cheerleading squad, but he had always thought the human pyramid was a neat routine. He never imagined, though, that he would have to climb up on somebody's shoulders in utter darkness.

"Ow!"

"Sorry!" Brian said.

"Just . . . maybe if I crouch down, and then you sit on my shoulders and I stand up . . ."

"I think I have to be actually standing on your shoulders for it to work. Look, just pretend you're a tree, and I'll climb you."

"Ow!"

"Sorry."

After several tries, with Roni getting crankier by the minute, Brian was finally able to balance on Roni's shoulders while she crouched down. That got him high enough that his head was almost inside the bottom of the shaft.

"Okay, now stand up," he said.

He felt her body shaking.

"You're too heavy!"

"No, I'm not. Just stand up."

"I can't. Your feet are trying to dislocate my shoulders."

"Hot bath," Brian said. "Fresh air, stop the bulldozers, French donuts, warm bed."

Roni groaned.

"Bats," Brian said. "The bats will be coming back." He felt around in the shaft and found a handhold. He would be able to take a little weight off her. "On three! One bat, two bats, THREE BATS!"

With a hoarse shout, Roni stood up, injecting Brian into the shaft.

As soon as he was in, Brian jammed his back against the wall and kicked one leg up to brace himself. Suddenly there was no Roni beneath him. He swung his other foot up and wedged himself firmly in the shaft.

Below him he heard Roni muttering to herself.

"Are you okay?" he asked.

"You kicked me in the head!"

"Sorry."

"Can you do it?"

"I think so," Brian said, even though he wasn't sure. He was afraid that if he moved even one of his feet off the wall, he'd crash down right on top of that pile of rocks and maybe Roni, too. But he had to try. He put his hands behind his back and pushed against them. Leaning forward, he started to walk up the wall. One hand, one foot, other hand, other foot. Inches at a time. If he slipped, there would be no rope to grab. He could see the stars above him, and soon he could see the rim of the shaft. Another few minutes of careful inching upward and he was able to touch the rocky rim. In one quick jerk he flung his arms over the edge of the hole and pushed as hard as he could with his feet. His chest hit the ground, and his legs were kicking in thin air. He stroked forward with his arms and wriggled out of the shaft.

"Brian?" Roni's voice sounded small and afraid.

"I'm out," he shouted back down.

"Is the rope still there?"

Brian looked around. The moon had risen, giving him enough light to see. He found the rope in a pile, still tied to the tree. He tugged on it to make sure the knot was secure, then dragged it back to the hole.

"The rope's coming down," he shouted.

He fed the rope into the hole.

"Got it!" Roni said.

"Think you can climb it?" he asked.

Roni didn't say anything. Several seconds passed.

"What are you doing?"

"Eating my Tootsie Roll."

"Don't forget about those bats," Brian said.

Silence.

A few seconds later Brian felt the rope go taut.

"Here I come," Roni said.

37

a drastic measure

They rolled to a stop in front of Brian's house. It was after one o'clock in the morning and all the lights were on. So much for sneaking in without his mom knowing he'd been gone. Brian swung off the Vespa and stood staring at the house.

Roni patted him on the back and said, "Good luck, Watson. I'm out of here."

Brian grabbed her arm. "No way. You're coming in with me."

"I won't be any help. Your mom doesn't even like me."

"She likes you. She just thinks you're a bad influence."

"Well, this is just going to prove it to her."

"If you're there, she'll have to listen. Besides"—Brian pointed at the car parked in the driveway—"correct me if I'm wrong, but isn't that your mom's car?"

Roni stared at the car.

"This can't be good," she said.

She climbed off Hillary and put her arm around Brian's shoulder. "Sorry, Watson, but this calls for a drastic measure."

"A what?"

Roni stomped on his foot.

"Ow! What was that for?"

"Limp," she ordered.

Their mothers were sitting at the kitchen table drinking coffee when Roni and Brian walked in, Roni supporting a limping Brian.

Mrs. Bain started by saying, "This better be pretty good—" But when she saw their dirt-streaked faces and Brian's pathetic limp, she jumped up and ran to him. "What happened, baby?"

Roni wanted to spit out, "Baby?" But she waited until they got Brian sitting in a chair, his mother fussing over him, to say, "He's fine, really, but we barely made it out alive."

"Out of where?" Nick asked, giving Roni a suspicious look. "Where have you two been?"

"We . . . um . . . well, I was doing this research on the Internet, and then Brian called and—"

"Roni! Focus! I asked you a question."

"We were solving a crime," Brian said.

"I should have known," said Mrs. Bain. "What was it this time? Murder? Genocide? Grand larceny?"

"Attempted murder," said Brian.

"Fraud," said Roni.

"Assault and battery."

"Unauthorized dynamiting."

"Fraud," said Brian.

"I already said *fraud,*" said Roni.

"It deserves to be mentioned twice."

"Hang on," said Mrs. Bain, holding up her hands. "Slow down. Back up. First things first. Are you two okay?"

Roni and Brian nodded.

"Why were you limping?" Mrs. Bain asked Brian.

"It's kind of a long story. See, a few hours ago I was thinking about bats, and—"

Roni looked from her mom's face to Brian's mom's face as they listened to Brian tell the story. They were both hooked. Now all they had to do was reel them in.

38

jailed

"The Bloodwater County courthouse was built of white granite in the year 1932," intoned Professor Bloom. He loved the sound of his own voice echoing in the cavernous space. The class had gathered in the courthouse lobby for the class on Bloodwater politics and government.

The professor moved off down the hallway followed by the class, their grubby sneakers and flip-flops shuffling along the marble floor. Bloom could see that they weren't particularly interested in what he had to say. Kids today were brain dead. Why had he agreed to take this demeaning job? Teaching high school students was like trying to swim up a waterfall. He heard a giggle behind him.

Bloom narrowed his eyes and glared at the pack of young fools. Sometimes a good staring down would silence them for a few minutes.

"Now, as I was saying, this is the political heart of the county, and—yes, Eric?"

"Roni and Brian aren't here yet. Maybe we should wait for them."

"If they are late, that is their problem," said the professor. "They will have to catch up on their own."

"I know Roni really wanted to see the jail."

"*Mister* Bloodwater, we are not here for Miss Delicata's

165

amusement, we are here to learn." He gave Eric an extra-hard glare, forcing the boy to look away. "Now, as I was saying, this courthouse has been the scene of many famous cases . . ."

The courthouse tour proceeded with no further interruptions from the students. Just as well that Roni Delicata was absent. That girl had been the source of constant disruptions with her frivolous questions. Professor Bloom much preferred his students silent and attentive. Silent, at least.

A small but determined-looking woman wearing a gray suit with an ID badge on her lapel was waiting near the entrance to the prison wing.

"Good morning, Professor," she said. "I'm Detective Bain."

"Ah! Detective Bain," said Professor Bloom. "Will you be escorting us through the jail?"

"Yes. I thought we could begin with the holding cells." She typed her code into a keypad on the wall. The door opened into a hallway lined on one side with barred ten-foot-square cubicles. "After you," said Detective Bain.

Professor Bloom walked through the door, followed by his class.

Eric Bloodwater sighed and watched the class file through the steel doorway into the county jail. He did not like jails. His parents had both been in jail once, and he was afraid that they would soon be in jail again.

"Hey, Eric! You coming or not?"

Eric looked up and forced himself to smile. "I'm coming," he said, and he walked into the jail, his shoulders slumped.

The detective was demonstrating how the locks on the jail cells worked. "They lock automatically when the door is closed," she said. "Anybody want to know what it's like to be in jail? If you're innocent, I promise to let you out."

Nobody volunteered.

The detective smiled. "A lot of guilty consciences out there. What about you folks?" she said, looking down the hall. Everybody in the class turned to see Roni, Brian and Mayor Buddy Berglund coming down the hall. The mayor was followed by a tall woman wearing a green pantsuit— Roni's mother, Nick.

"Sorry we're late, Professor," said Brian. "Roni and I had to make a run out to Indian Bluff this morning."

"Indeed," said Professor Bloom, scowling.

"Come on, now, doesn't anybody want to experience jail firsthand?" asked Detective Bain.

"Why don't you try it, Eric?" said Roni. "You could use the practice."

Eric felt his heart go *thump*. He said, "Huh?"

"Oh, for pity's sake, I'll go in," said Professor Bloom. "My conscience is as pure as driven snow!" Professor Bloom entered the jail cell. "There," he said, crossing his arms.

Roni stepped forward and slammed the jail cell door.

"There," she said.

"Ha ha," said Professor Bloom. "You can let me out now."

"Ha ha," said Brian. "I don't think so."

Professor Bloom darted an irritated glance at Brian, then did a double take.

"Young man, what on earth do you have on your face?"

39

a permanent complication

"This?" Brian popped the black rubber cup off his nose. "Just a little something I found in a cave. Why?"

Professor Bloom's face darkened. He thumped his cane on the cell floor and looked at Brian's mother. "Detective Bain, I'm sure you find this very amusing, but I must insist that you open this door immediately!"

"I'm sorry, Professor, I can't do that," said Detective Bain. "It seems you might be guilty of something after all."

"Me? Don't be absurd!"

Detective Bain took the black rubber cup from Brian. "Do you recognize this, Professor?"

Professor Bloom sniffed. "It appears to be the tip from a cane."

"It's the tip from *your* cane," Roni said.

"Ridiculous!" He held up his cane. "As you can see, my rubber tip is firmly attached to my cane."

"Yes, but on the first day of class your cane *had* no tip," Roni said. "You lost it that morning, before class, in the cave at Indian Bluff. It must have popped off when you hit Dr. Dart."

Professor Bloom opened his mouth to speak, but no sound came out. All the blood seemed to drain from his face. "You can't prove a thing."

Detective Bain reached through the bars and snatched the professor's cane. "Our forensics people will examine your cane for microscopic traces of blood or hair, Professor. I wonder what they'll find."

"I bet you'll also find his footprints in the cave," Brian added.

Roni said, "You attacked Dr. Dart, and then you blew up the cave entrance so nobody else could go in there. And you tried to trap me and Brian in the cave after we found another entrance!"

The professor backed farther into the cell and sat down on the thin cot. "No," he said, staring down between his long legs at the concrete floor.

"Yes," said Roni.

Professor Bloom's head snapped up. "You foolish, meddlesome child. You think you know everything. You know nothing! I had nothing to do with sealing up that accursed cave. And as far as Andrew Dart is concerned, he deserved what he got!"

"And why is that?" asked Detective Bain in a quiet voice.

"All Dart cared about was dead things. Bones and stone tools. The man was a ghoul. He cared nothing for the living plants. If it were up to him, those detestable condominiums would be built down on the river bottoms, destroying countless trout lilies and rare lady's slippers. I could not allow that!"

"So you tried to kill him?" Brian said.

"I was just trying to slow him down."

"And you tried to kill us, too!" said Roni.

The professor sniffed. "I knew you'd find a way out. And if you didn't, who would miss you?"

"I would," said Brian.

"So would I," said Eric.

Roni felt herself blush.

"At least my trout lilies are safe," said the professor, crossing his arms. "The bulldozers have no doubt already begun construction on the bluff!"

Mayor Berglund cleared his throat. "I'm afraid that is not true, Professor Bloom. There has been a slight, um, delay in the Indian Bluff development. A complication, as it were."

"A permanent complication," added Nick.

Roni looked at Brian. They smiled at each other, remembering their early morning meeting with the mayor. Roni had shown him the article she had pulled off the Web, and the mayor had immediately called the contractors and told them the Indian Bluff project had been canceled.

"You mean . . ." The professor seemed to collapse in on himself. "But what about the plants? My beautiful trout lilies?"

Roni, despite all the professor had done, took pity on him. "Your plants are safe, Professor. The condominium project has been canceled. It seems that the Bloodwaters aren't Bloodwaters after all."

Brian asked, "Where did you get the dynamite to blow up the cave, Professor?"

Professor Bloom shook his head. "I blew up nothing," he said. "I abhor loud noises. I am a man of peace."

"Tell that to the judge," said Detective Bain. "Now, it's time for me to pay a call on Mr. Fred Bloodwater—or whatever his name is." She clapped her hands. "Class dismissed!"

Roni turned to look for Eric . . . but he had disappeared.

40

bindweed seeds

"That was really pitiful," said Brian. "All the guy wanted to do was save his precious trout lilies."

"Yeah, by trying to do away with three people, two of who were us."

"I think it's 'two of *whom*.'"

"You sure it isn't 'two of *which*'?"

"I have no idea—you're the writer." Brian was walking with one foot in the gutter and one on the curb. *Up, down, up, down . . .*

"Why are you walking like that?" Roni asked.

"Why?"

"Because it looks stupid."

. . . up, down, up, down . . .

"I don't mind looking stupid."

"I've noticed that."

"Hey, you know what was the coolest thing that happened this morning?"

"Slamming the door on Professor Bloom, for sure."

"Nah. It was the expression on Mayor Berglund's face when you showed him that article."

Roni grinned. "That *was* pretty cool."

"I noticed that Eric disappeared as soon as you started talking about the Bloodwaters."

"Your mom's probably arrested the whole family by now."

"I doubt it. They haven't actually done anything wrong yet. At least not here in Bloodwater. The mayor froze Bloodwater Development's bank account. Fred Bloodwater never had a chance to make off with the money."

Brian stopped walking. Mercy Hospital rose to their left. "You ready?"

In one way, Dr. Andrew Dart was feeling much better. He was able to recognize the doctors and nurses, he could sit up in bed without his head spinning and he remembered most of what had happened to him at Indian Bluff—finding the cave and the skeleton . . . but he didn't remember much that had happened after that.

But in another way, he was feeling much, much worse. However, it helped that Jillian was sitting next to him, holding his hand, wearing his ring.

"Today is the day, isn't it," he said.

Jillian Greystone nodded. "The bulldozers were scheduled to raze the bluff this morning. I'm sure they've got it half torn up by now."

Dr. Dart shook his bandaged head sadly. "Such a tragedy. So much important archaeological data lost forever."

Jillian produced an exasperated sputter. "Andrew, there is absolutely no evidence that Indian Bluff was ever occupied by Native Americans. You have *got* to accept that. I walked that entire area and didn't find so much as the chip off a projectile point."

"But they *must* have lived there! It's the perfect spot. What about the skeleton I found? What about the turkey tail?"

"Andrew, Andrew, Andrew . . ." Shaking her head, Jillian stood up and went to the window. "I know you filched that turkey tail from our collection at the college. I tracked it down."

Dart felt his head detaching again. He lay back on his bed and ordered the ceiling to stop spinning. What could he say to make Jillian understand? He didn't want to lose her again.

"I just wanted some time. If I could have delayed the construction, I just *know* I would have found something. And I really did find a skeleton in there!"

"You sure did!" said a new voice.

Dart turned his head to find two familiar young faces standing in the doorway. Where had he seen them before?

"Do I know you?" he asked.

"These are the kids who found you in the cave," Jillian said. "Roni Delicata and Aston LaRue."

"Actually, my name is Brian," said Brian.

"How are you feeling, Dr. Dart?" asked Roni.

"Much better, thank you," said Dr. Dart.

"He's upset about the bulldozers," said Jillian.

Roni and Brian looked at each other and grinned.

"What's so funny?" asked Dr. Dart.

"No bulldozers," Roni said.

"We stopped them," said Brian.

"Actually, it was mostly me who stopped them," Roni said.

"But I'm the one who found the cane tip."

"But I'm the one who knew what it was."

"And I figured out about the bats."

"But I—"

"Hold on," said Dr. Dart, sitting up in his bed and waving his hands. "I have no idea what you two are talking about!"

"The development has been canceled," Roni said. "We found out that the developer was a con artist."

"And we found out that it was Professor Bloom who attacked you in the cave," Brian added.

"Bloom! Why on earth would that tree hugger want to hurt me?"

"He was afraid you might find something on the bluff that would cause the development to be relocated to his precious river bottoms."

Andrew Dart sat blinking, trying to take it all in. "So my bluff is safe? The skeleton is still there in the cave?"

"Not exactly," said Brian. He shrugged off his backpack, unzipped it and reached inside. "I want you to meet an old friend." He pulled out a yellow skull and set it at the foot of the bed. "Say hello to Yorick."

Dart's eyes bulged. "Young man! Don't you know that you should never remove archaeological evidence from its point of origin?"

"I don't think this exactly qualifies as archaeological evidence, Dr. Dart." Brian turned the skull around so Dr. Dart could see the back of it.

"What on earth is that?" asked Dart, staring at the shiny metal patch on the back of the skull.

"It's a metal plate in his skull. He has gold fillings in his teeth, too," said Brian.

Dr. Dart's jaw fell open.

"I think maybe your Native American is not so native after all," said Roni.

As they were leaving Dr. Dart's hospital room, a thin dark-skinned man wearing a turban flagged them down.

"Young man!"

"Hi, Dr. Singh," said Brian. "It looks like Dr. Dart is doing better today."

"Very much so, thanks to you!"

Roni had no idea what was going on.

"What did I do?" asked Brian.

"You're the one who noticed that Dr. Dart had those seeds in his mouth!"

"I thought they were rocks."

"They turned out to be seeds of the bindweed plant, a type of wild morning glory. It seems these seeds are highly toxic and hallucinogenic. It was no wonder the doctor was raving!"

Roni said, "You mean he was eating seeds that made him see things?"

"Apparently so," said Dr. Singh. "Once we knew what the problem was, we were able to flush out his system. He claims to know nothing about where the seeds came from."

Brian said, "Do you remember a tallish fellow with a cane coming to visit him?"

"A fellow with bulgy eyes and a pouchy sort of lip?"

"That would be him."

Dr. Singh frowned. "He visited Dr. Dart every day."

Brian and Roni exchanged a look.

"Professor Bloom!" they said with one voice.

41

fenton

"I guess we know now why Professor Bloom was visiting Dr. Dart," said Roni.

"Yeah. He was feeding him hallucinogenic bindweed seeds so everybody would think he was crazy, " Brian said. "At first, Dr. Dart was all messed up cause he got hit on the head. Professor Bloom wanted to make sure he stayed that way by feeding him the seeds." Once again, he was walking with one foot in the gutter and the other on the curb. *Up, down, up, down.*

"Better that than bonking him again with his cane."

"I bet he was the one who blew up the cave entrance, too."

"But why would he deny doing that after confessing to attacking Dr. Dart?"

"Who knows? Maybe Professor Bloom was eating some of his own seeds."

"I guess it doesn't really matter," Roni said. "He's going to jail either way. And would you please stop walking like that? It's embarrassing."

"I'm not embarrassed. I'm celebrating. Professor Bloom is in jail, Mayor Berglund is the one who's embarrassed, the so-called Bloodwaters are done for and Dr. Dart just found

179

out that his ancient Indian is some dude with a metal plate in his skull. I call that a good day!"

"I wonder who he was," Roni said.

"Who?"

"Yorick."

Brian shrugged. "Probably just some homeless person who crawled into the cave to die."

"Oh well, I guess we can't solve every mystery in Bloodwater."

That night, Roni had to listen to yet another lecture from her mother on the Dangers of Caves, and the Perils of Going Out Late at Night, and assorted other Parental Concerns.

"When I think of you trapped in that cave, with those bulldozers above you—why, that entire cave system might have collapsed!"

"Don't forget the bats," said Roni. "I could've got rabies, too. Or starved to death. With rabies."

"Exactly," said Nick. "Which is why I think we should let that horrible motorcycle sit in the garage for the rest of the summer—"

"Hillary is not a motorcycle, Nick. She's a motor *scooter.* Besides, I was getting in trouble long before I got Hillary."

"That's true," said Nick.

"Besides, if you take Hillary away, you're going to have to *drive* me everywhere."

Nick frowned, considering.

"And I never actually got in trouble while I was *on* Hillary."

"Not yet, you haven't," Nick said.

The discussion lasted for several more minutes, ending with Nick saying, "We'll see . . ." Which was as good as Roni could have hoped for.

Brian was sitting at the kitchen table having a similar discussion with his mother.

"No computer—"

"Mom!"

"No bicycle—"

"Mom!"

"No skateboard, no—"

Brian reached into his backpack and pulled out Yorick, hoping to distract his mother from her list of deprivations. It worked.

"Good Lord, Brian! Where on earth did you get that?"

"Mom, this is Yorick. Yorick, this is Mom."

"Brian, what on earth—did you go back into that cave?"

"I had to, Mom! I had to show it to Dr. Dart. But I thought you should see it, too. It's not an Indian, see?" He turned the skull to show her the metal patch.

At that moment, Mr. Bain came into the kitchen to see what all the commotion was about.

"Is that the skull from the cave, son?"

Brian nodded.

"Congratulations!" said Mr. Bain.

Both Brian and Mrs. Bain looked at him, confused.

"Congratulations? Why?" Brian asked.

"You've solved Bloodwater's oldest mystery!" He picked up the skull and examined it. "Farley Bloodwater," he said. "This is the metal patch they put in his skull after he got conked by that chandelier." He turned the skull and looked into its empty eye sockets. "Long time no see, Farley!"

Roni lay in bed staring up at her ceiling, trying to stop the slide show in her head.

What would happen to Professor Bloom? What would happen to Eric and his family? Was the condominium project permanently canceled, or would the college just sell the land to some other developer? And if Professor Bloom hadn't blown up the cave entrance, then who had?

Roni's thoughts were interrupted by the rattle of pebbles hitting her bedroom window. She ran to the window and looked down to see Eric Bloodwater's face looking up at her. Thirty seconds later, Roni was sneaking out the back door in her flannel poodle pajamas.

"Hey, Poophead," she said.

"Hey," Eric said, smiling. "My real name's Fenton, you know."

"I like Eric better."

"Me, too. I didn't pick the name Fenton."

"I didn't pick Petronella."

"Petronella? That's your real name? You never told me that!"

"Now that you know, I'll thank you never to use it."

Eric laughed. "I guess you stopped my dad from building those condos."

"I guess. Only from what I've read, he'd never have gotten around to actually building them."

Eric shrugged. "My dad is kind of a dreamer."

"More like kind of a crook."

"He's not a bad person. He just loves to come up with these grand schemes, but he doesn't so much like the part where you actually have to *build* it."

"Yeah, but why does he have to steal people's money?"

"We have to live on *something*."

Roni looked down at the black poodles frolicking on her blue pajamas. She wasn't often at a loss for words, but right now she didn't know what to say.

"I just came to say good-bye," he said.

"I figured," Roni said. "Where will you go?"

"I have no idea." He grinned. "But maybe I'll send you a postcard when I get there."

"I'd like that."

"I have to get back. The moving van should be all packed by now. Oh, one more thing . . ."

"Yeah?"

"That was me that blew up the cave. I was just trying to save my dad's project. I stole the dynamite from the contractor's trailer. They were going to use it to blow up some stumps. I'm sorry." He turned and walked quickly away, in the direction of Bloodwater House.

Roni watched him go, wondering if Brian's mom knew the "Bloodwaters" were about to skip town. Would she care? Probably not. Fitzroy Oraczko may have been a crook, but in this case he hadn't gotten around to stealing the money yet.

Roni shook her head, let herself back into the house and went to bed.

42

indian bluff revisited

Two weeks after Professor Bloom's final class, Brian's mother finally relented on her "no bicycle" rule. The first thing Brian did was ride out to Indian Bluff. He wasn't sure why. Maybe he just wanted to see it again without the bulldozers and orange surveyor's stakes.

It was a perfect summer day, warm, dry and slightly breezy. Big puffy cartoon clouds floated overhead. He rode his bike up to the edge of the bluff and looked out across Professor Bloom's precious bottoms. He wondered how the professor liked sitting in his concrete cell without a plant in sight.

Brian set his bike down and walked along the edge, remembering the night he and Roni had spent in the cave. One of these days he'd get some good caving equipment and go back down there.

He heard the sound of a motor. Looking up, he saw Roni puttering across the field on her Vespa.

He waved, and she steered toward him.

"How you doing, Sherlock?" Brian said.

"Very well, Watson. You here to relive past glories?"

"I guess. What about you?"

"I came to get the rope we left behind. Mr. Billig wants it back."

"That was a good rope. So, any new mysteries on the horizon?"

"I'm sure something will crop up."

Brian kicked at the ground with the toe of his sneaker. As he did so, he noticed a leaf-shaped rock. He bent over and picked it up.

"Hey," he said.

"Hey what?"

Brian held up a pale, rose-colored stone. It was pointed at one end, forked at the other and the edges had been carefully chipped to razor sharpness.

"Is that what I think it is?" Roni asked.

Brian smiled. "I believe it is."